Rise of the Living Dead

SHAUN HARBINGER

One

I FELT LIKE I WAS dying.

Mike and the girls strode on ahead of me, backpacks bobbing up and down as they marched up the mountain. They didn't look back. They had decided long ago, almost as soon as we left the cars and began this trudge up the mountain, that I was just slowing them down. They were right. If we did this hike at my preferred pace, the speed would be much slower than this kamikaze attack on the Welsh landscape. As it was, every step sent excruciating pain lancing through my leg muscles. My breath hurt as it rasped into my lungs, bringing with it the afternoon mist that might have tasted fresh if I could stop gasping for air like a fish out of water.

And that's exactly what I was. This gung-ho shit was Mike's deal, not mine. He and Elena spent most weekends hiking or rock climbing or canoeing down some river somewhere. I spent my weekends playing video games and eating fast food. Most of the Chinese, Indian and Mexican restaurants knew the way to my house. The pizza guy had almost become a close friend because we spent so much time talking about the latest games while he was delivering my pepperoni feast and garlic bread.

After spending weekdays at my shitty admin job, I needed to unwind during my two days of freedom.

He might have been my closest friend, despite our differences in lifestyle, but Mike's outdoor weekend pursuits were my idea of hell. Even though he and Elena spent a lot of their time having wild sex in the remote locations they visited, it was still too much torture for a few moments of pleasure in my eyes.

So if that's what I thought why the hell was I here now, torturing myself just to try and get to know Lucy Hoffmeister?

Because I was a fucking idiot who should know better.

When Mike told me that Elena was bringing her friend Lucy along for a two day trek of Wales, and would I like to join them, I was playing Day Z and had just eliminated two zombies and another player who had been bugging me for weeks in-game. I had been on a digital high. An image of Lucy Hoffmeister had flashed across my mind and I had said hell yeah. The image that incited this uncharacteristic reaction was one of Lucy at Doug Latimer's barbecue last year. Lucy had arrived with Elena and I had spent most of the evening trying not to stare at her. She was perfect. Cute face, button nose, blue eyes and long blonde hair which tumbled over the shoulders of her black sweater. She filled that sweater and her jeans with just the right amount of curves.

I didn't talk to her, of course. Nothing more than a hello when Mike introduced us. Girls like that don't go for geeks like me. I knew I had no chance with her. Even now, struggling up this mountain while she laughed and talked with Mike and Elena up ahead, I was aware that the differences between us were an abyss that could not be crossed.

But the image of Lucy at Doug Latimer's house, to be exact a particular image of her in the kitchen grabbing a bottle of beer, popping it open and leaning her head back while she took a swallow from the bottle, had the power to bring me here to this godforsaken place and put myself through hell. In that moment, Lucy had seemed totally unaware of the effect she had on all the men at that barbecue. I was leaning against the kitchen counter when she took a swig of that beer and I took the opportunity to let my eyes roam over her from head to toe. That view of her standing by the fridge, leaning on her right leg a little more than the left so her hip curved out more on that side, her perfect breasts thrusting against the black fabric of the sweater, was a memory I had replayed over and over in my head many times.

That image and my Day Z victory had betrayed me. I wasn't meant to be here. This was not how I spent my Saturdays. I should be at home right now, controller in hand and a beer on the coffee table. And my own bed to sleep in tonight, not a cold uncomfortable tent. I was going to feel like hell by the time I went back to work on Monday.

And up ahead on the steep trail, the three happy wanderers ambled up the mountainside, chatting like this was a stroll in the park. I was huffing and puffing like a steam train. How could I be so out of shape? Mike was loving this, flanked by two girls while he showed off his physical prowess. Never mind his friend coming up half a mile behind everyone else, trying to not have a heart attack but at the same time wishing he were dead. I didn't want them to wait for me. That would mean exerting myself to reach them faster while they watched me. Too embarrassing. Let them get ahead as much as they wanted. They had to stop sometime. Then I would catch up at my own pace.

For now, I would just trundle along behind them and wish I was someplace else.

When they finally stopped for lunch, I almost lost them.

They reached the top of the mountain and disappeared from my sight as I scrambled up after them, driven on by the knowledge that this constant uphill struggle was about to come to an end. As I topped the trail and looked out across the broad rocky area that marked the zenith of this mountain, the three amigos were nowhere to be seen.

I let out a breath and a muttered, "Fuck." Relieved to be on level terrain but worried that I was lost, I walked forward a few steps and scanned the mist around me. There were dark shapes moving in the gray, figures just out of sight, but they were other hikers in pairs and in large groups, not the three who had left me on a mountainside.

I unzipped the pocket of my jacket and took out my phone. I would have to call Mike to find out where they were. Embarrassing, yes, but not as embarrassing as being airlifted off the mountain by the Mountain Rescue people because I had gotten totally lost.

There was no signal. This was a joke.

Putting the phone away, I considered the other type of calling, actually shouting for them. But the presence of the other hikers, the same ones who had passed me on the way up here and offered sympathetic smiles and nods, stopped me. I didn't want to look like a total loser.

So I marched over the rocks and tried to look like I knew exactly where I was going.

Right past everyone else and over to the other side of the mountain.

At least the next part of this trek was going to be downhill.

It seemed pointless, struggling up a mountain just to go back down again.

"Alex, over here."

I halted and looked to my left. Sitting behind a pile of rocks, sheltering from the wind, Mike, Elena and Lucy waved at me. They had filled plastic mugs with steaming coffee from the Thermos. It smelled so good it made my mouth water.

I strode over to them swinging my arms and trying to look strong, as if doing so could make them forget about me lagging behind for the entire morning.

"Grab a drink, Man, you look beat." Mike passed me a mug and poured coffee into it.

The breeze blew the steam into my face. Looking at Elena and Lucy, I said, "You girls enjoying yourselves? It's pretty wild up here."

"Yeah, it's cool,' Elena said. "We were thinking of picking up speed on the next part. You up for that, Alex?"

She knew I wasn't. I had been half a mile behind them the whole way and my bravado a moment ago hadn't really made them forget how pathetic I was. I shrugged.

"We don't have to pick up the pace," Lucy offered.

Mike swallowed his coffee and threw the dregs across the rocks. "We do if we want to make camp before dark. Alex will be OK." He took a plastic-covered map from his rucksack and laid it on the ground. "Look," he said to me, "we head from here to the top of Pen Y Fan. Then down to this area where we skirt around this mountain called the Cribyn. Once we get around there we can put up the tents."

"Why are you showing me the map? I'll just follow you."

"In case you fall too far behind and lose us. Now you know where we're going."

His directions and random pointing at the map hadn't told me anything. "You could just slow down a little," I whispered.

"No way, Man. You try to keep up. This is good for you, Alex. The military come here all the time. This is where the S.A.S. train."

As if on cue, an army helicopter flew overhead. Couldn't they take me to the Cribyn or whatever the hell it was called and drop me off there? I wouldn't mind waiting while Mike and the girls caught up. I'd even try to set up the tents.

"I'm not a soldier," I said. "I thought this was supposed to be enjoyable, not a military exercise."

Mike stood up and stowed the mugs in his backpack and stood up. "Just pretend it's Call Of Duty," he said, hefting the pack onto his back and adjusting the straps. "You can keep up if you try harder, Alex."

The girls got ready to leave with Mike. I scrambled to my feet. My legs protested but I tried to ignore the ache in my muscles. Keeping up with the group would be difficult but getting lost out here on the middle of nowhere, especially when it got dark, would be a nightmare. I doubted I could survive a night wandering around the mountains.

"Everyone ready?" Mike asked. "Let's go."

He took off like a mountain goat across the rocks.

The girls joined him and I followed along. At least I had a pretty good view walking behind the girls.

We descended a steep jumble of rocks then found a path that led up to the summit of Pen Y Fan. My three non-companions hit their stride again and powered ahead.

I slowed down. There was no point trying to keep up and my legs screamed in pain with every step. I unzipped my jacket and reached into the inside pocket. I had my portable digital radio in there along with a Twix bar.

Unravelling the headphone wire and pushing the buds into my ears, I switched on the radio. At least I could have some music to take my mind off the ache in my legs. I could have listened to music from my phone but I didn't want to run the battery down so I had turned it off after unsuccessfully trying to call Mike earlier.

I unwrapped the Twix and bit off a mouthful. The sweet caramel taste seemed amplified out here in the wilds. It was probably because I hadn't eaten since we left the cars hours ago. The sweetness seemed to explode in my mouth.

The radio was nowhere near as satisfying. Instead of music, all I got was a news broadcast and the signal kept cutting out. As I trudged up the path I tried to make out what the woman was saying.

"Department of Health issued a warning after…at the Royal London Hospital…virus strain that…previously unknown…a doctor has been quarantined…no danger to the public."

I flicked the radio off, disconnected it from the headphones, and stuffed it back into my pocket. Leaving the headphones in my ears, I jacked them into my phone and turned it on, finding an AC/DC album on my playlist. Screw the battery, I needed some distraction from this hell.

Trying to let my awareness of the rock music override the awareness of my aching legs, I strode on along the trail, leaving the shadowy figures of the other hikers behind me in the mist.

The driving rock beat helped me forget the pain in my legs for awhile, or at least endure it. It lifted my spirits. Took me away from the misty damp reality of the mountains. I decided that I was going to talk to Lucy tonight. To hell with it.

What did I have to lose?

This was already the worst Saturday of my life.

It couldn't get any worse.

I reached the top of Pen Y Fan. Nothing spectacular, just more rocks and a cairn to mark the pinnacle. I looked for the path down the other side and found it easily. Things were looking up despite the fact I couldn't see Mike and the girls anywhere. Going down the mountain was much easier than going up even though my feet ached. I couldn't wait to get my boots off later. As unappealing as the tent sounded, compared to this endless trudging it would be luxurious.

A noise in the mist brought me to a halt.

I heard it over my music. It had been loud. Like someone falling over.

I took off my headphones and listened.

Another noise. It sounded like a growl.

It couldn't be. There weren't any dangerous animals up here.

What about a dog? Maybe some idiot hiker had brought a Doberman up here and let it off the leash.

The growl reached me again. Low, guttural.

I swallowed.

If it was a dog, surely the owner was around somewhere. Maybe that was who had fallen over.

I heard movement. To my right. It didn't sound like a dog. Not unless dogs wore padded jackets and carried rucksacks and walked in boots.

It was a hiker.

Maybe it was the owner looking for his dog.

So why wasn't he calling for it?

I heard another noise, behind me this time. A group of hikers coming down the trail chatting and laughing. Maybe they would know how to deal with a dangerous dog.

The growl came again.

Then a quick movement. A man. Coming out of the mist.

His face. Oh God, his face!

He reached out for me with both hands, his yellow eyes looking like pure evil. His skin was blue, mottled, disgusting. Pure instinct sent me running backwards away from him, dodging his flailing arms.

The heel of my boot connected with a rock.

I tried to regain my balance.

Fell.

Hit the grass.

Air rushed out of my lungs in an explosion.

RAIN

My vision filled with sky and dirt.
Tumbling.

Two

I SCRAMBLED TO MY FEET, stifling the cry that rose in my throat. I didn't know how far I'd rolled down the mountain but I wasn't going to wait around for that crazy guy to come down after me. I ran.

Not strictly true. It was impossible to run because of the steepness of the slope. I loped down the trail, letting gravity speed me up. Not too fast. I couldn't risk hurtling down the mountain.

There were no sounds behind me. All I could hear was my own breathing. I sounded like a panting dog. What if he heard me?

Maybe those other hikers would deal with him.

Or maybe he would deal with them. He looked crazy. Murderous.

I should call someone. Mountain Rescue. The Police.

Turning off the music on my phone, I tried to decide what to do. I didn't even know the number for Mountain Rescue and what would I tell the police?

I called Mike. Luckily I got a signal.

"Hey, Alex."

"Mike, where are you? I... I don't know what's happening. I just got attacked by some... someone."

"Hey, slow down, Man. Are you OK?"

"I don't know. Yeah, I think so. I got away."

I heard him tell Elena and Lucy, "Alex got attacked by somebody."

Then Lucy's voice came sweetly into my ear. "Tell him we'll wait for him."

"Yeah, we'll wait for you, Man. We can't be too far ahead of you. We'll wait here until you catch up."

I hung up and put the phone away. I wasn't in the mood for music anymore and I couldn't risk not hearing that mad hiker if he was still coming after me. I glanced back up along the trail. Nothing but mist.

Then a shout. A scream. A roar of anger.

I fled as fast as I could.

I hit level ground and kept running across the grass. My lungs burned. Tears streamed out of my eyes and I wasn't sure if I was crying or if the exertion was making them water. My mind was filled with pure panic. He had found the hikers behind me up there. Killed them. Surely the sounds of screaming meant he was killing them. And when he was done, would he come down after me?

Three shapes appeared in the mist ahead of me. I slowed down and approached carefully. What if that madman wasn't alone? What if there was a cult of killers? I had seen that on a TV show I couldn't remember the name of right now. If there were three of them, I had no chance. I couldn't run anymore. I was done.

"What happened, Man?" Mike's voice had never sounded so good.

I went over and leaned on him, panting, trying to catch my breath. "I... there was... mad hiker... attacked... fell."

"Whoa, Man. Take it easy."

Lucy and Elena looked more worried than Mike. I don't think Mike would be worried if was abducted and woke up in the trunk of a serial killer's car. He'd probably wait until the killer opened the trunk then give him a shit-eating grin and say, "You don't want to kill me, Man."

And knowing Mike's luck, the killer would probably reply, "Yeah, you're right," and let him go free.

Knowing *my* luck, I'd probably suffocate in the trunk before the killer even opened it.

I managed to get my breathing from panicked to just heavy. "There's a crazy person back there," I said. "He attacked me but I tripped over a rock and rolled halfway down the mountain. I got away but there were some other hikers behind me. I... I don't think they made it."

"What? Are you sure?"

I shrugged. "I couldn't see anything because of the mist but I heard screams."

"Ah," he said, "screams of terror or surprise? Maybe they knew the guy. Maybe he jumped out of the mist to scare them. He thought you were them and he jumped out at you by accident."

"It was no accident and the screams were screams of terror. I'm not stupid, Mike. He really attacked me. His face…" I tried to recall exactly what his face had looked like. "The flesh was blue. His eyes were yellow."

"Sounds like you got attacked by a smurf."

Elena laughed.

Lucy spoke up for me. "Come on, this is no laughing matter. Alex looks scared. What if there really is a crazy person back there?"

Mike tried to look serious but I could see he didn't believe me. He was such a dick at times. "Then I guess you should call the police, Man. And we'll have to wait for them to arrive. You'll need to give a statement. They'll take forever asking you questions. It's already getting dark. I don't want to be putting up the tents at midnight."

"What if I call them anonymously? I just tell them what happened and hang up. They'll come out to investigate but we'll still get to the camp site on time."

He shrugged. "Sure thing. Just don't stay on the line too long. We need to get moving."

"I won't." I dialled '999' on my phone and waited, listening to it ring at the other end.

I waited two minutes. There was no answer. "I thought this was supposed to be the emergency services."

"Maybe they're busy," Lucy offered. "It's Saturday night. They probably get busy on the weekend."

I hung up and redialled. The phone at the other end rang and rang but nobody answered. I looked at the screen of my phone. Everything looked fine and I had a signal. "There's nobody there."

"I'll try on my phone." Lucy took her phone from her pocket and dialled. She flicked her long blonde hair from her ear as she placed the phone there. I didn't hang up, letting the ringing go on and on. Lucy listened to the same thing on her phone for at least three minutes before she hung up. "Nothing."

"Well we need to get moving,' Mike said. "You can try later." He set off along the path.

I caught up with him. "You don't think it's strange that the emergency services number isn't working?"

He shrugged. "Like Lucy said, they're probably busy, Man."

Elena took Mike's arm and looked at me with something like pity in her eyes. "Don't worry, Alex. The world isn't ending."

I sighed and dropped back to where Lucy was marching behind them. She gave an occasional glance into the mist behind us. She at least she believed me. "Don't you think its weird that there's no answer from the emergency services?" I asked her.

"It's strange. Maybe it's because the signal is bad here."

"But I could hear the ringing sound. I was connected."

"Maybe there's a fault on the line or something." When she saw frustration on my face, she added, "We could try again later."

"Something doesn't add up," I said. In fact, I was hoping it *didn't* add up because if there was a connection between the strange radio broadcast earlier, the mottled blue skin and yellow eyes of my attacker and the fact the emergency number was dead, then something was seriously fucked up. Get a hold of yourself, Alex, maybe this is just a bunch of unconnected incidents. Maybe you've been playing too many video games and you aren't thinking clearly. This unfamiliar environment has affected you, not to mention the fact that you are walking next to Lucy Hoffmeister right now.

That thought drained all my confidence away. My throat went suddenly dry. I had talked to her easily a moment ago because my mind had been on other things. Now that I thought about talking to her, I couldn't do it.

She sensed my discomfort and looked at her phone, pretending to be interested in something on the screen.

I took out the radio and turned it on. The station crackled and emitted white noise. I rotated the tuning dial, seeking a voice from the outside world. There were no live stations.

"The signal here really is bad," Lucy said.

"It isn't that. See that green indicator? That means the radio is tuned to a digital channel. There's just nothing on the channel."

"Try a different one."

I adjusted the tuner.

A woman's voice came through the static. Her intonation was flat, as if she were reading from a script. "This is the BBC emergency broadcast. Stay in your home. The military and police are dealing with the current situation. Stay inside and lock all doors and windows." A pause then the recorded message was repeated. "This is the BBC emergency…"

I ran up to Mike. "Listen." I turned up the volume.

"…And police are dealing with the current situation. Stay inside and lock all doors and windows."

"What the fuck, Man?"

"It's the Emergency Broadcast System. They only use it if something really fucking bad has happened. We've got to get home. We can't be out here in the middle of nowhere if something's happening."

He stopped and looked me in the eyes. "Alex, is this a joke? Some sort of prank?"

I shook my head. "I swear it isn't." The EBS continued to repeat on a loop.

"Turn that fucking radio off."

I did so gladly. I couldn't stand to listen to it any longer.

"Maybe it's a test," Elena suggested. "They test these things all the time, right? They have to know it works in case they need it in a real emergency."

"Yeah, they do that all the time, Man. They close underground stations and practice for biological warfare and shit like that."

"Not on every station. I can't get anything else at all on the radio. No music, no news, nothing."

He took out his phone and jabbed at it. His eyes flickered over the screen and his face went pale. "Oh fuck," he muttered.

Elena put her head on his shoulder and looked at his phone."What is is, Mike?"

"There hasn't been an update on the internet news channel since two hours ago. It just says 'Virus Outbreak.' Nothing else. There's nothing else." He pressed the screen on his phone a few times. "I can't get shit on here."

"We need to go back," I said.

"Alex is right," Lucy added.

Mike ran his hands through his hair and paced back and forth on the trail. "We should keep going. Make camp. It's a lot further back to the cars then it is to the camp site. If… if the shit really has hit the fan we might be in the best place out here. It's getting dark and it's going to rain. We need to set up camp. Come on." He stormed off down the trail. Elena went running after him.

Lucy looked at me. "What do you think?"

"He's probably right. If we went back to the cars now, it'd get dark before we got anywhere near them. I don't fancy walking over the mountains in the pitch black."

"Me either."

We set off after Mike and Elena. Lucy was quiet for awhile, lost in her own thoughts, but then she asked, 'Alex, what do you think has happened?"

"I don't know. If it's a virus, how could it spread so quickly? I heard a news report earlier that mentioned a hospital in London and a doctor in quarantine. But when we left home this morning, there was no mention of anything on the news."

She went quiet again then said, "I'm scared."

I looked at the darkening sky.

Something told me this was the end of the last normal day ever.

Life was never going to be the same again.

Three

W E SET THE TENTS UP quickly. The trail led us around the side of the mountain Mike called the Cribyn then to a flat area of grass where we would spend the night. Mountains surrounded us and a rocky ravine ran off down a steep slope. It felt isolated. If the world had gone to hell, isolated could be good.

As we put together the steel poles and threaded them through the nylon loops as quickly as we could, I tried to piece together the fragments of knowledge I had. A viral outbreak. All media dead except for the emergency broadcast. A warning to lock all doors and windows.

It was that last fragment that scared me.

If a virus had somehow broken out from a London hospital, even if that virus was deadly, why were they telling people to lock their doors?

My mind went to places I didn't want it to even consider going.

The infected.

Whatever this virus was, it had already spread enough to take out the radio stations and the internet. Was it worldwide? None of us could get any internet on our phones. In theory, that might just mean that the service providers in this area were down.

Or it could mean that the whole world was affected by the virus.

We erected the first tent and I looked at the flimsy fabric dome held together by hollow steel tubes. No protection. Not from the infected.

Jesus Christ, Alex, stop scaring yourself.

But even Mike had gone silent. He moved on to the next tent and started fitting the poles together. He had brought two tents, one for the boys and one for the girls. We placed them close together. It doesn't matter how close they are, I thought, if someone comes up that ravine and attacks us, we're as good as dead. Huddling together like frightened animals won't help us.

I imagined a horde of infected men and women with blue skin ripping at the tents with sharp nails and teeth. Not stopping even when those nails and teeth were ripping flesh.

"Alex."

I looked up. "Yeah?"

"Let's get inside. It's starting to rain."

I nodded.

We shoved our rucksacks in one tent and the girls' in the other. Mike and I climbed into ours and zipped up the door just as heavy drops of rain hit the tent. Slowly at first then faster. Like a thousand fingers drumming on the fabric.

We unrolled the sleeping bags and laid them out on the tent floor. Mike lit a kerosene lamp and hung it from a hook on the ceiling.

"You girls OK in there?" he shouted.

"We're fine," Elena replied.

He looked at me. "Alex, I don't think there's really anything wrong. There's something wrong with the internet, yeah. And the radio. But we're in the middle of nowhere out here, Man. That's life in the sticks for you. Fuck all communication."

"What about the emergency broadcast?"

"You must have tuned in to some military test channel or something. I told you, the army train up here all the time. We're probably in the middle of one of their war games or something. Yeah, that makes sense. That explains the media blackout. There's like a jammer or something to simulate a war." The more he thought about it, the more he seemed to convince himself.

I thought about what he was saying. Was it plausible? The army did come to these mountains to train, particularly the S.A.S. who were based at Hereford not too far from here. But surely even they would put up signs telling hikers they were blocking the local phone towers wouldn't they? Maybe not. My knowledge of military matters was limited to video games. I had no idea if they would even consider how their training protocols affected civilians.

"I think you could be right," I told Mike. After all, even my game-addicted mind acknowledged that scenario was more likely than some sort of zombie outbreak. It was the army. We had seen their choppers earlier so they were definitely in the area. I breathed a little easier. It made sense.

"Hey, girls," Mike called, "I've figured it out. The world isn't ending after all. It's the fucking army playing around."

"What do you mean?"

A smirk crossed his face. "I'll come in there and explain it to Elena. Alex will explain it to Lucy."

"What?" I whispered.

"Hey, Man, I spent the last few hours thinking the world was ending. Now I know it's not, I need to do something life-affirming, if you know what I mean."

"Mike, no." I didn't care what he did with Elena, it was the fact that Lucy was going to come into this tent that scared me.

He patted me on the shoulder as he left the tent. "Just talk to Lucy. She likes you, Man."

I sat back on my sleeping bag, leaning against my rucksack. I had agreed to come on this trip in a moment of weakness, thinking I would get to know Lucy Hoffmeister and maybe have a chance to go out with her. That moment had long since passed and I knew in the cold light of reality that I didn't have a chance with Lucy. I wasn't good at talking to any girls, particularly good-looking ones. I wasn't scared of them or anything like that, I just got tongue-tied and embarrassed around them. So I went quiet. Then they thought I disliked them because I wouldn't speak to them.

On my twentieth birthday, Mike had taken me to Amsterdam with a couple of his friends and they had paid for a certain lady in the red light district to help me become a man. She didn't speak English and I didn't speak Dutch so my communication problem didn't become a factor.

Mike thought the experience would help me overcome my shyness with women when we returned back home but as soon as we got off the plane, I was back to my old self. The worst thing about it was, I didn't want to be this way. I wanted normal relationships with girls. I wasn't proud that I had lost my virginity to a prostitute. I would rather have a real girlfriend.

The door unzipped and Lucy climbed into the tent. She looked as embarrassed as I felt. She would probably rather be anywhere than in a tent with me.

"Hey," I said.

"Hey." She sat on Mike's sleeping bag, facing me. She had tied her hair up into a pony tail and taken off her jacket. Sitting there in beige cargo pants and a black sweater, she looked even sexier because I had the impression she didn't acknowledge her own sexiness. The understated makeup, tied-up hair and curves refusing to be hidden by the loose sweater accentuated the beauty Lucy was either unaware of or was trying to play down. The pale light from the lamp made her look ethereal.

"Mike said he's figured out what's happening," she prompted, probably aware of my eyes on her.

"He came up with an explanation and it makes sense. We're probably in the middle of some war game. The S.A.S. train up here all the time. The emergency broadcast, the lack of signal, it's probably part of their training."

"What about the man who attacked you?"

"Maybe it *was* just a guy in a mask trying to scare his friends. I didn't stick around long enough to find out." But that explanation sounded lame. His eyes had burned with such fury. Those yellow eyes still haunted my thoughts. Even if the rest was a military exercise, it didn't explain the man on the mountain.

"You don't sound so sure."

I shrugged. "Let's try the radio again. There might be a better signal here." I rolled onto my stomach and pulled the radio out of my jacket where I had draped it over my rucksack. I clicked it on.

Lucy got onto her stomach next to me, her blue eyes on the radio. Our hips and shoulders were touching. I could smell her light perfume. Concentrate, Alex.

Static filled the tent. I turned the dial slowly. Silence. Then a voice. "This is the BBC emergency broadcast. Stay in your home. The military and police are dealing…"

"It's the same broadcast," Lucy said. "It must have been playing all day. Over and over."

I searched for more stations but got nothing. Turning off the radio, I said, "So what do you think? Are we in the middle of a very realistic military training exercise or is this for real?"

She looked at me and there were tears in her eyes. "I think it's real."

Her conviction made me realize I had been fooling myself. This had to be real. If the army wanted to train their soldiers and deny them media access, they would simply take away their radios, phones and any other devices that allowed access to cyberspace. They wouldn't blackout the entire area.

"I think you're right," I admitted. That admission broke through a dam that had been holding back the emotions inside of me. I thought of my parents, my brother Joe. My friends. Were they safe?

Reflecting my thoughts, Lucy asked, "What about our families?" Tears rolled down her cheeks.

"I don't know," I said.

"Please hold me." She pressed herself into me.

I turned so we faced each other, her head buried against my chest. Her arm went around my waist and I put mine around her shoulders as we both cried in the pale lantern light. This was it. The end. Something had happened to finally put an end to society as we knew it. This was real.

Game over.

Four

WOKE UP WHEN SUNLIGHT hit the tent and the birds started their chorus outside. Just like any other day. Just like yesterday. But yesterday was gone and all we had to look forward to was a very different tomorrow. I opened my bleary eyes to find Lucy asleep next to me. Somehow we had fallen asleep last night and ended up tangled together in the sleeping bags. Her head was on my chest, her eyes closed. She looked so peaceful. My arm was trapped beneath her body and it felt dead. My back ached from sleeping on the ground all night. The sleeping bags had hardly provided a layer of comfort.

I moved gently, dragging my arm from under Lucy. I extricated it and waited while the blood returned, sending pins and needles shooting through my hand and fingers. The tent smelled of sweat and tears with an undercurrent of Lucy's perfume. I sat up. It was cold. At least the rain had stopped.

Crawling to the tent door, I unzipped it and climbed out into the chill morning. There was no sound from Mike and Elena's tent so I assumed they were still asleep.

Thick mist shrouded the tops of the mountains and also drifted along the ground. It was like one of those old horror movies where the set was covered in dry ice.

Apart from the calling of the occasional bird, there was no other sound. I staggered across to the ravine, rubbing my aching back, and relieved myself behind a tree.

It was too quiet. Could this silent world really be a place in which some event happened yesterday, some diS.A.S.ter?

In the distance, a helicopter whirred. It came up along the ravine. The dull green paint job distinguished it as military. The men in that chopper probably knew what the hell was going on. As it passed over us, the noise from its rotors seemed to fill the air, killing the silence.

Mike appeared, looking up at the sky, his eyes bloodshot. The helicopter passed over us and continued on over the mountains. As it disappeared into the distance, the unnerving quiet settled over us again.

Mike came over to me. He was wearing just a t-shirt and boxers. He must be freezing but he didn't seem to notice the cold.

"Dude," he said as he approached, smiling, "how was your night? Mine was fucking awesome."

Ignoring his question, I said, "We've decided it's real, Mike. The warning. Everything."

"For fuck's sake, not this again. So now you've convinced Lucy with your paranoid delusions."

"I'm not paranoid."

"Like fuck you aren't, Alex. You couldn't just come out here and have some fun could you? You had to go and turn it into one of your games. You can't just come out here and hike around the mountains for a couple of days, you have to make it the end of the fucking world. Well here's some news for you. This is just a normal day like any other. Tomorrow you'll be back at work like every other Monday. Same old shit as always. So let's enjoy today and make the most of it."

"Mike, we think it's real."

He glared at me and shook his head. "You really are crazy." He stalked back to the tents and picked up a saucepan and spoon. Crashing them together, he shouted, "Come on, ladies, it's time to get up and get moving. We have to go home today."

Elena and Lucy appeared, blinking against the sunlight.

"Let's get all this packed up." Mike's attitude was brash and loud. "Got to get back to the cars by this afternoon. Move it, people!" He tossed the pan and spoon into the grass. They clattered as they rolled across the grass then went silent. Mike walked away from the tents and stood staring up at the misty mountains.

I went over to him and put a hand on his shoulder. "Mike…"

He shrugged me off and took a few steps away. His eyes had tears in them. I had never seen Mike cry. Never.

"You'll see," he said, waving a finger at me. "We'll get to the cars and go home and everything will be just fine. And we'll be telling this story in the pub with our friends, telling them how Alex thought the fucking world had ended. And they'll laugh and drink to your paranoid delusional fucking conspiracy theories."

I went back to the tent without a word. Climbing inside, I shook my head.

"What is it?" Lucy was rolling the sleeping bags up.

"Mike doesn't believe us. Except maybe he does but can't admit it."

"What do you think we'll find when we get back home?"

"If something really bad has happened, we won't make it home, Lucy. If there's a virus, the army will have checkpoints, quarantine. They'll try to separate the infected. I suppose they'll set up emergency hospitals."

"But we're not infected."

"No, but they won't know that. They'll probably put people in quarantine for the duration of the incubation period of the virus. That's the only way they could separate the healthy population from the infected. Unless there's a blood test or something."

"This is so fucked up."

"Look, maybe we're wrong. Maybe we'll get back home and everything will be normal like Mike says."

Neither of us believed that.

We packed up the tents and gear into the rucksacks and left the campsite, heading along the hiking trail as it ran through a sharp-smelling pine forest. Mike had said we should be back at the cars by late afternoon. After saying that, he had gone quiet, walking ahead with Elena while Lucy and I trailed behind. Our little group, which yesterday had been split by physical fitness, was now split by beliefs.

The shadows among the pines made me think of the man who had attacked me yesterday and one word kept repeating itself over and over in my mind: infected. If the people infected by the virus became violent, that would explain the warning on the EBS to lock all doors and windows.

Lucy was quiet as we walked, her mind obviously on her family and thoughts of home.

I hoped that whatever was happening, my parents and Joe were OK.

Mike and Elena stopped and waited for us. As we reached them, Mike said, "I'm going to prove to you that nothing's wrong, Man," He pointed past the edge of the forest to a farmhouse on a hill. "They must have a TV in there. We'll go ask them if anything is wrong. They'll think we're crazy but at least it'll make you shut up about your crazy theory."

I looked a the place beyond the pines. It looked deserted. Apart from a few sheep grazing in the field, there were no signs of life. But Mike was right; at least we would know for sure what had happened.

We left the trail and made our way through the trees to the wooden fence that skirted the farm. After throwing the rucksacks over into the field, we climbed over one by one. The fence may have been strong enough to keep sheep in the field but didn't look like it could take our combined weight. As I slipped the rucksack straps back onto my shoulders, I took a better look at the farmhouse.

An old building made of wood which had seen better days, it had two levels and was flanked by stables and a barn. There was a faded blue Land Rover parked on a patchy areas of grass by the house. Looked like someone was home after all.

The others had already started for the house so I jogged to catch up with them. The sheep weren't too happy about strangers in their field and moved as far away from us as they could get, watching us with baleful yellow eyes.

"This place looks creepy," Elena said as we got closer to the house.

"It's just run down," Mike replied. "Anyway, it will solve the mystery of the end of the world once and for all."

We climbed the fence and stood before the place. Mike strode up onto the wooden porch and knocked on the door.

Lucy wrinkled her nose. "What's that smell?"

As soon as she said it, I smelled it too. Like dead, rancid meat. Probably a dead animal the farmer hadn't disposed of yet.

"Jesus, Alex, you could have waited," Mike joked, knocking on the door again.

"I don't think anyone's home," I said.

"Maybe they've been evacuated," Lucy offered.

"Oh for fuck's sake." Mike tried the door and it opened. "OK, let's find the TV." He stepped inside.

"We can't just go into someone's house," Lucy said.

"Hey, the door was open. If that isn't an invitation, I don't know what is." He disappeared inside.

Elena followed.

Lucy looked at me. "Should we go in?"

"We want to know what's happened. There might be something on the TV."

She nodded and stepped through the door.

I followed, not oblivious to the fact that a split had occurred in the group and Lucy was on my side. It felt good.

The house looked like it had last been decorated sometime during the seventies. Peeling wooden panels adorned the hall and garish green and yellow wallpaper covered the walls of the living room. The sofa and chairs in there were covered in green paisley fabric. In the corner, looking out of place among the retro decor, stood a big flat screen TV. Mike found the remote and turned it on.

The screen popped into life, showing us a message that simply said, 'Off Air'.

"Try another channel," Elena suggested.

Mike flicked through the channels. Each had a different message but all said essentially the same thing.

Off air.

Not transmitting.

Dead.

"This isn't fucking happening, Man," Mike said, throwing the remote against the sofa. It bounced off the cushions and landed on the carpet. The battery hatch lid broke off and the batteries spilled out like tubular guts.

"You can't be thinking what they're thinking," Elena said to Mike.

He looked at her. "What else is there to think? No TV. No radio. Some fucked up message on every channel." He looked over at me. "I think you're right, Man. I hate to say it but I think you're right."

"Mike, no." Elena shook her head. "This can't be happening."

He looked at me. "Tell me about this virus."

"We don't know much. Something about a doctor being quarantined in a hospital in London. I think the infected are dangerous. That's why there was a warning on the radio to lock all doors and windows."

He nodded grimly. "Try the radio. I want to hear that message again."

I took the radio out of my pocket and switched it on. The familiar voice filled the room. "...emergency broadcast. Stay in your home. The military and police are dealing with the current situation. Stay inside and lock all doors and windows. If law enforcement or military personnel come to your home, do as instructed and proceed to the checkpoint they designate. Do not open your door to anyone except law enforcement or military personnel. Do not leave your home unless instructed. This is the BBC emergency broadcast. Stay in…"

I switched it off.

"What's all that about checkpoints?" Mike asked.

"It didn't say that yesterday. They added that part."

"Fuck."

"No, that's good. It means the army and the police have a plan. They're dealing with the situation. Sending people to a safe place."

"And what about us?" Elena asked. "Are we in a safe place?"

"We're far away enough from the shit that's going down to be safe," Mike replied.

I shook my head. "No, we're not. What about the man who attacked me yesterday? He must have been infected. The people who live out here still go into populated areas to get supplies, to go shopping. They come into contact with the rest of society all the time. Where are the owners of this farm?"

As if in reply, a noise came from upstairs. It sounded like someone climbing out of bed and walking across the wooden floor. The floorboards creaked with each step.

Mike looked up at the ceiling. "There's someone here, Man." His voice had dropped to an urgent whisper.

Elena's eyes were wide with terror. "What do we do?"

The footsteps upstairs creaked slowly across the room and sounded like they were moving toward the stairs.

"I'm getting out of here." Mike ran for the front door and out of the house.

"Let's go," I said to the girls.

Elena went next, then Lucy. As I reached the bottom of the stairs, I glanced up to the floor above.

There at the top stood the farmer. Dressed in blue jeans and a red check shirt that had a dark blood stain across the shoulder. His skin was mottled blue and his eyes were yellow. He drew back his lips and snarled.

He stepped down onto the top step. His eyes looked more like a wild animal's than a human's.

And they looked at me with pure rage.

I fled the house but as soon as I got outside, I heard a sound that pierced the morning air.

Lucy screaming.

Five

I SQUINTED AGAINST THE SUN as I ran out onto the porch. Lucy and Elena stood flattened to the wall of the house, their frightened eyes locked on the scene in front of them.

Mike was lying on the ground face down, hands behind his neck. Above him stood a soldier pointing an assault rifle at Mike's head. The man was dressed in green combat gear. His black hair was close-cropped and his face looked hard.

I halted on the porch, aware of the creaking stairs behind me. The farmer was coming down slowly but it wouldn't be a moment or two before he was within grabbing distance of me. I moved away from the open doorway.

"Stay where you are," the soldier said. "How many more of you are there?"

"None," I said. "But I really need to move. There's an infected person in there."

He narrowed his eyes. "What do you know about the infected? Has one of your group been bitten?"

Another creak on the stairs. A low moan.

"It's the owner of this house," I said quickly. "Please, I have to move. Don't shoot me."

"Stay where you are or I'll shoot your friend. Don't even think about stepping away from that doorway."

Lucy glanced sideways at me, her big blue eyes gleaming with tears. She must have seen what was behind me because they opened even wider and she screamed.

A low groan sounded behind me. The farmer was almost at the bottom of the stairs now.

The dead meat smell got stronger, making me want to vomit.

If I ran, the soldier would shoot Mike then the rest of us. If I stayed where I was, the infected farmer was going to kill me.

"Please…" I begged the soldier.

"Don't you move," he ordered.

I closed my eyes.

The farmer reached the bottom step. He was in the hallway now.

I heard his footsteps coming closer.

The smell was overwhelming.

Mike, his face still in the dirt, pleaded for me. "Please, let him move away from the door. Please."

The soldier looked down and told Mike to shut up.

Bang

The gunshot came from behind me, from inside the house. I felt something wet hit the back of my jacket.

The farmer collapsed to the floor with a heavy *thump*.

I looked over my shoulder. A second soldier came from the kitchen, looked down at the farmer and nudged the body with the toe of his combat boot. "We need to get rid of this thing, Cartwright. It fucking stinks."

He stepped out onto the porch and looked us over. "Back inside, everybody. There's a whole bunch of Nasties coming this way and I don't think you want to be outdoors when they get here." He looked over at his companion. "Let him up, Cartwright. He isn't going anywhere."

Cartwright stepped back, allowing Mike to get to his feet.

We went back into the living room while the soldiers dragged the farmer's body out of the house and into the grass.

They came back inside and closed the front door behind them.

The soldier who seemed to be in charge came into the room and said, "Right, listen up. My name is Sergeant Brand. You can call me Mr. Brand or Sergeant. Anything else will get you shot. I am in charge. If you want to live, you will accept that. Ladies, close all the curtains in the house. Gentlemen, find the keys and lock the doors."

We did as he said. Mike and I went into the kitchen looking for the house keys. We found them hanging from a cast iron rooster on the wall next to the back door. As he locked the door, Mike whispered, "Do you think we can trust them?"

"We don't have a choice at the moment."

"What happened to the farmer, Man? He was like a fucking zombie."

"All the more reason to trust these soldiers. They have guns. If there are more of those things out there, we don't stand a chance without weapons."

We walked through to the hallway to lock the front door. Lucy and Elena stood at the foot of the stairs. Brand came out of the living room. "What's wrong, ladies?"

"We don't want to go upstairs," Elena said. "That's where he came from."

"Cartwright, check upstairs."

Cartwright went up, rifle raised.

Brand looked at me. His eyes were steel grey. "You need to wash your jacket. Got some blood and brains on the back there. What's your name?"

"Alex."

"Well, Alex, once Corporal Cartwright has cleared upstairs, you need to wash your jacket in the bath. It stinks of death."

"What regiment are you from?" I asked. Neither man wore any identifying insignia. They didn't even have stripes on their arms to designate rank.

"We're from *the* Regiment, lad." He winked at me.

"What does that mean?" Mike asked.

"S.A.S.," I said. "They're from the S.A.S.."

"I didn't say that," Brand said lightly, "If I told you that, I'd have to kill you." He winked again.

"Clear," Cartwright shouted down from upstairs. "There's a hell of a mess on the bed, though. I reckon he was lying there when he turned."

Lucy and Elena went up to close the curtains.

I followed them. I needed to get the pieces of farmer off my jacket.

* * *

With the house in darkness, Cartwright lit a fire in the fireplace with logs he found next to the wood-burning stove in the kitchen. The flickering flames lent the room an eerie orange glow. My cleaned-up jacket hung in the hall drying along with everyone else's. We were making ourselves at home as much as possible but we all kept our boots on, knowing we may need to make a quick escape from the house.

Brand and Cartwright had removed their combat jackets. Beneath, they wore dark green army sweaters over green shirts. They sat near the window, occasionally pulling back the curtains to peek out. They kept their weapons close.

"Can you tell us what's happened?" I asked Brand.

He looked surprised. "You don't know?"

"We were in the mountains. All we know is what the EBS says. I heard something about a virus but my radio wasn't working properly."

"There is a virus. One fucked up virus. Yesterday morning, India went dark. No communication from inside the country at all. Nothing. There had been reports for a few weeks about a new outbreak of bubonic plague there. You know the black plague that killed off most of England in the middle ages? Well that plague still exists in India. So nobody thought much of it.

"There were some strange reports coming out of the country about infected people going mad but this all happened in the mountains, in the villages. Then yesterday, the entire country went off radar. People over here tried to contact relatives there, the newspapers had news crews out there but suddenly there was no word coming back from them. Nothing.

"Then it turns out a doctor in London who had been working in the mountain villages for a couple of months and returned to Britain last week got put into quarantine three days ago. Whatever had been killing people off over there was now over here. Fucker brought it back with him. By the time they got him into quarantine, it was too late. He was already dead."

He took a glance out of the window then turned his face back to us. "He was dead but still trying to attack people. He managed to bite a nurse and a paramedic. Probably already infected people in his street before they took him to hospital.

"By Saturday lunchtime, the police were overrun with emergency calls. People being attacked on the street. Loved ones suddenly taking ill."

He shrugged. "You can guess the rest. It's a virus. It spreads itself by making the host bite the uninfected. It's like one of those late night films. Who'd have thought they'd have hit the nail on the head when it came to the end of the world?" He shook his head as if in disgust.

"The world?" Lucy asked. "Is it really the world?"

He looked at her and nodded. "That doctor wasn't the only person coming out of India on that flight. There were other flights that flew from there all over the world before the country's lights went out. The virus has gone worldwide."

Even though I already knew something terrible had happened to society, having it confirmed made me feel sick. I tried to imagine the chaos and panic spreading across the world, through all the cities, through every neighborhood, every street.

"What about survivors?" I asked, remembering the addition to the emergency broadcast.

"We're doing all we can," Brand said grimly. "The hospitals are under military command. We've set up checkpoints along all major traffic routes to try and contain the virus in certain areas. We're not winning the battle. The infected are a big problem. They move slowly but they're bloody determined. And they move in groups. So if you shoot one there are ten more still coming at you. We're trying to keep the survivors safe while also fighting the Nasties. It's a losing battle. Especially when the survivors you save have a nasty habit of turning into Nasties themselves."

"They're here," Cartwright said, peering out through the window.

"Everybody keep quiet," Brand whispered.

I could hear shuffling outside, movement in the grass, Then a heavy set of footsteps sounded on the wood of the porch and I felt adrenaline pumping through my body. I wanted to run but there was nowhere to run to.

Another set of footsteps joined the first and the two Nasties lumbered along the porch. A bang on the door made me jump. It sounded like a fist landing heavily on the wood.

A pause then another bang.

Then another.

Cartwright whispered, "I count seven of them out there."

"There are some around the back as well," Brand replied.

As if to prove him correct, a heavy fist landed on the back door.

Knock knock.

"Can they get in?" Lucy whispered.

Brand shook his head. "They're testing for ways into the house but they aren't intelligent enough to combine their strength to break the doors down."

Something hit the window at the back of the house and we all jumped. Another blow to the glass made it shudder in the frame.

Brand positioned himself so he faced the window, assault rifle ready in case the thing outside broke through.

As they pounded on the doors and windows, Lucy looked at me with fear in her eyes. "I can't take much more of this."

I put a comforting arm around her shoulder.

"Do they know we're in here?" Mike fidgeted nervously by the fireplace. He looked like he might actually run out of the house and into the mountains. His body trembled with unspent adrenaline and his eyes darted around the room every time one of those things banged on the house.

"Who knows?" Brand shrugged. "They probably know that people live in houses so there might be people inside this one. If they don't get in and we don't make a noise, they should move on. They respond to movement and sound. If they don't see or hear anything that attracts their attention, they go elsewhere."

We sat there in the glow of the firelight while the zombies shuffled around the house and tested the doors and windows. We probably sat like that for half an hour but it seemed like an eternity. When the banging and pounding stopped, Cartwright and Brand still didn't touch the curtains in case the Nasties were still in the area.

When Brand finally looked out, he said, "They're gone."

The entire room breathed a sigh of relief.

Brand pulled back the curtains to let light spill into the room. "Now how about some food? There must be something in that kitchen."

"I'll see what there is," Lucy said, getting up.

"I'll come with you." I got to my feet then froze when I heard a sound on the window.

Brand laughed. "You scaredy-cat, it's just the rain."

The sky opened and heavy droplets of rain spattered against the glass, In the distance, thunder rumbled.

"Typical Welsh weather," Cartwright murmured.

"Yeah, but it gave our lad here a fright." Brand laughed again and Cartwright joined him.

Following Lucy into the kitchen, I tried to ignore the laughter. We had all just sat here hiding from a bunch of zombies so it was no wonder I felt on edge. I was still coming down from an adrenaline high.

Lucy rummaged through the cupboards and found pasta. Placing it onto the kitchen counter, she searched in another cupboard and brought out two jars of sauce. There was a wood-burning stove sitting in the corner but also a modern gas cooker on one wall. I took two saucepans from the wall where they hung from metal hooks and filled one of them with water before placing it on the burner and turning on the gas. The ignitor sparked and the gas lit with blue flame, heating the water. I found a salt shaker and added a few grains to the pan

Outside, the rain came down heavier, lashing against the house from a dark grey sky. The view from the kitchen window showed open grassy fields leading to the mountains.

"What are we going to do, Alex?" Lucy placed the pasta into the boiling pan of water.

"What can we do except try to survive?"

"We can't stay in this house forever." She stirred the pasta with a fork.

"Where else can we go?"

"What about our families? You have a brother don't you? And your parents are still alive?"

They were the last time I checked but I didn't hold out much hope now. "Yeah, I have a brother. Joe. He's two years older than me and when we were growing up he was a pain in the ass but we get on much better now we don't live in the same house."

I didn't realize it at the time but when I was younger, Joe looked out for me. A lot. As a geek, I got pushed around in school, made fun of by the other kids, avoided by most of the girls.

I found out a few years after leaving school that Joe had gotten into a few scrapes on my behalf, including a fight that saw him taking on the school bully Derek Green. I remembered Joe coming home with a black eye and bruises but he never told me until we were both adults that he had fought with Green that day because the bully made a remark about me. I didn't even hear him say it but Joe went wading in to defend me.

I prayed to all the gods in heaven that Joe was still alive somewhere, surviving this shit. It didn't seem right for me to be still alive if Joe was dead. He was tough and I was weak. He was successful in life but I was mediocre.

"Don't you want to know what happened to him?" Lucy asked.

"Of course I do. But what can I do about that right now? It's not like I can just go to his house and say, 'Hey, Joe, what do you think of all this zombie stuff?' while he makes me a cup of tea. He won't be there. I just hope he's with our parents. They lived quite close. Maybe Joe had time to get to their house before all the virus stuff went too crazy."

"We're going to have to find our families sometime," she said, looking out of the window at the rain.

"Yes, but we also have to stay alive. We're safe here."

She stared at the stormy landscape. "For now. What happens when those… Nasties… realize we're in here?"

"That's not going to be a problem," Brand said from the doorway. "You can't stay here. Why do you think Cartwright and I are here? We're doing a sweep to gather the remaining uninfected survivors for the Survivors Camp at Brecon."

"But we don't want to go to a Survivors Camp," I said. I had a problem with authority and the thought of being herded into a military camp with a load of other people, some of whom could be infected, sounded worse than trying to survive alone.

"You don't have a choice," Brand said. "We're in charge now. The Government has declared a state of emergency. Britain is controlled by the military. Don't worry, there's a checkpoint on the main road. We'll get you there safely. I hear the camps aren't too bad."

"I'm not going to any camp," I said.

"We can't have you running about out here. Look at you. You'll get turned in no time, then it's one more Nasty for us to deal with."

"I'll take my chances."

He looked at me with a hard stare and shook his head. "No, you won't. Either we escort you civilians to the checkpoint or we take you there at gunpoint. It makes no difference to us." He looked at Lucy and winked. "How's that food coming along, Gorgeous?"

"It'll be ready in ten minutes," she said, turning to the stove and stirring the pot so she didn't have to look at him.

"Excellent." He went back to the living room.

Lucy looked at me and whispered, "What are we going to do?"

"I don't know." What chance did we have against two armed special forces soldiers? If we tried to run, they would shoot us. As far as they were concerned, we were dead out here anyway. They wouldn't hesitate to pull the trigger. If we went with them, we would be trapped in a military-run camp with hundreds of other survivors. A concentration of people like that would be too big an attraction for the zombies to ignore.

One thing I knew: the camp would mean death for us all.

We had to take our chances surviving on our own wits. If a steady diet of zombie movies and books had taught me anything, they had taught me that the military and the government were fallible. Eventually, they would get everyone killed either through ignorance or through over-confidence in their own abilities. I didn't want to get killed just because some organization made a fatal mistake while my life was in their hands.

If I was going to die, it would be on my own terms.

I went over to the key hooks where we had found the house keys. Hanging there was a set of keys with a leather Land Rover key tag attached to them. I took them from the hook and placed them in my back pocket.

Lucy saw what I was doing and nodded.

I nodded back.

The keys were a secret shared between us.

We were getting out of here.

Six

THE MEAL TASTED GOOD. THE tomato sauce was infused with garlic, peppers and herbs and Lucy found some cheese in the fridge which we melted on the pasta. The kitchen was filled with the aroma of Italian sauce. As the six of us sat around the table eating, we were silent. The only sound was the rain hitting the roof and windows.

I was hungry and the food helped curb the gnawing in my belly. I didn't want to talk, I needed to think. How were we going to get away from the soldiers while we had the chance? Only Lucy and I knew about the Land Rover keys in my pocket. I wanted to tell Mike and Elena but there was no way I could do that without Brand and Cartwright overhearing.

When we were all done, every scrap of pasta had been eaten. Brand pushed his chair back and stood up. He looked at Cartwright. "Right, we need to get these civvies to the checkpoint."

Cartwright nodded and wiped tomato sauce from his lips with a napkin.

"We're OK as we are, Man," Mike said.

Brand sighed. "I already had this conversation with your friend here. You're civilians. You have to go to the Survivors Camp. Leave fighting the zombies to us big boys."

"Maybe we'll be safe there," Elena said.

"See, your girlfriend's got some sense. Now let's go."

My mind raced for a way to escape. We couldn't just make a run for it, we'd have no chance. Brand would gun us down before we reached the back door.

We all stood solemnly, like prisoners of war about to be taken for execution.

After we had our jackets and rucksacks on, Brand looked us over.

"It's about a mile to the main road," he said, "so stick with us. Don't get any ideas about running away because I *will* kill you. If you're not going to the camp, you're just another Nasty as far as I'm concerned. Cartwright, have a look out of the window and see if any of our dead friends have come back."

Cartwright went into the living room and glanced out. "Just rain and mountains out there."

Brand nodded. "You lead the way and I'll bring up the rear."

Going over to the front door, Cartwright unlocked it and stepped out onto the porch.

And all hell broke loose.

He took two steps over the threshold, rifle pointed ahead of him, and was about to step from the covered porch into the rain when a shape lunged out from beside the door. Cartwright turned, his face a mask of surprise.

The shape was a zombie. A hiker dressed in hiking gear and with a backpack slung over his shoulders. He roared as he stepped toward Cartwright, his arms outstretched.

Cartwright spun on his heels, firing point blank into the zombie's head. Blood and brains blew over the porch and the hiker dropped backward.

But as soon as he fell, four more took his place.

Two old women, one of them dressed in a white bathrobe which fell open as she lurched forward, showing me more of her blue mottled flesh than I wanted to see, and two young men who looked like they were farmers judging by their beards and flannel shirts, fell onto Cartwright, dragging him across the porch by his boot.

Brand jumped out through the doorway and started firing in three-round bursts, his teeth gritted as he took aim and fired. His training made his movements almost automatic.

He grabbed Cartwright's jacket and pulled him back inside.

"Shut the door!" he shouted. "There are more of them out there!"

Mike slammed the door shut and locked it.

"They were out there waiting for us," Brand said, shocked. "They were fucking waiting for us!"

Cartwright sat propped against the stairs. Blood oozed from his calf. He stared at the floor as if in a trance.

Brand saw the wound and cursed. He tore a strip of fabric from Cartwright's torn combat trousers and tied it above the wound. "It's gonna be OK, Dave," he muttered. "It's gonna be OK."

"They bit me," Cartwright said simply. "I got bit. It hurts."

A heavy thump sounded against the front door.

Then another.

A barrage of banging assaulted the flimsy wood. It sounded like they were throwing their bodies at the door, trying to break in.

Brand stood and wrenched the door open, sending a spray of bullets out through the doorway. Two more zombies fell. Behind them, at least a dozen more clawed at Brand. He fired into the mass of rotting flesh, his roar of anger louder than the sound of the assault rifle as it spat bullets.

He closed the door again, leaning his back against it, breathing hard.

The banging started again.

Cartwright's eyes were closed, his head drooping.

Brand looked at his companion and something inside him seemed to snap. He pulled the door open again and began firing.

I took the others into the kitchen. "We need to get out of here. Brand is going to get us all killed."

In the doorway, Brand was kicking and screaming at the zombies, sending hailstorms of bullets into their rotted flesh.

A movement at the foot of the stairs caught my attention. Cartwright twitched, raised his head. His skin had changed and taken on a blue hue. The veins in his neck and face stood out like dark purple gnarled branches. His eyes were yellow, his glare hateful.

I tried to shout out to Brand but it was too late. Cartwright was on him, pushing the soldier out onto the porch even as he sunk his teeth into his neck.

Brand screamed.

His rifle clattered to the ground among the shuffling feet of the zombies that surrounded him.

They pulled him down, hungry mouths gnashing, nails clawing.

Some of them looked in our direction, left their prey and stumbled forward into the house.

We ran to the back door and unlocked it. It opened onto a grassy area beside the house. It looked empty. The only sound was the hissing of the rain.

Mike went out first. He turned toward the back of the house.

"No," I said. "The Land Rover. I've got the keys." I dug into my back pocket and grabbed them.

Mike changed direction and headed for the front of the house. We followed. My brain screamed at me to run away from the zombies but if we really wanted to escape, we needed the vehicle. Running blindly into the mountains would only get us into more trouble. If we had the Land Rover, we could travel faster and we had some protection.

Mike went around the side of the Land Rover and ducked down, waiting for us. I ran for the driver's door and pressed the unlock switch on the key fob. The doors clicked open.

We slipped our rucksacks off and piled in. I got behind the wheel and fumbled the key into the ignition. Only when the engine had roared into life did I risk a glance at the porch. The Nasties watched us with their yellow eyes but they didn't come for us. Lying at their feet, I saw the remains of Sergeant Brand and I felt acidic bile rise in my throat. Looking away, I reversed the Land Rover away from the house and spun it round so we faced the dirt track that led to the road. I put the windscreen wipers on at full speed. They sluiced the water from the screen, giving me a rain-smeared view of the track and the forest on either side.

The fence we had climbed over earlier was broken down in places, the wood splintered like broken bones.

I put the Rover into first gear and we drove out of the farm.

On either side of us, zombies stood in the trees, their angry eyes watching us as we passed.

Seven

E HIT THE MAIN ROAD and I turned right. The roads in this area were never busy but now they were deserted and it felt eerie. The tarmac stretched off into the distance and all we could see was rain, mist, mountains and trees. There were no other vehicles. It made us feel conspicuous being on the road alone.

"Why the hell didn't they follow us?" Mike asked from the passenger seat. He had found a road map in the door pocket and was looking for side roads that might lead us out of the area. If we stayed on the main road too long, we would hit an army checkpoint and be right back where we started; headed for a Survivors Camp.

I pulled over onto the side of the road, keeping the engine running. The farmer must have filled the tank before he fell ill because the fuel gauge read 'Full' and there were two jerry cans tied to the metal roof rack. I hoped they weren't empty but I wasn't about to leave the safety of the vehicle and check. I felt like we were exposed out here.

"I don't know why they didn't come after us," I said. "The ones that came into the house didn't follow us out of the back door either."

Mike tracked his finger along the map. "There's a right turn up ahead, Man. That takes us to Swansea. It's a main road but we can get off here and take the back roads."

"Why do we want to go to Swansea?" Elena asked. "We should stay away from cities. If there are loads of those things out here, imagine how many of them there are in the cities."

"We don't want to go to a city," I said. Then a thought occurred to me. "Maybe we should go in that direction, though. Swansea is on the coast. If we head Southwest, we'll come to the sea."

Lucy knew where I was going with that thought. "A boat," she said. "We can take a boat."

Mike grinned. "That's a sweet plan, Man. Those things would never get us on a boat." He slapped his leg and laughed. "Fuck yeah, let's go."

"There's a few miles between us and the sea," I said. "We don't know what we're driving into."

"Alex," Mike said, looking at me, "you've had a downer on this trip ever since we left home. Lighten up."

"Lighten up? I just nearly got eaten by fucking zombies."

We all laughed. The relief of getting away from the farm hit us and we expressed that emotion in laughter. Despite the fact that we were anything but safe, we forgot for a moment that the area was crawling with the undead. It felt good. A moment of the old world creeping into this new fucked up one.

I pulled back onto the road and set off slowly, looking for the right turn and keeping an eye out for checkpoints. A few miles along the road, we reached the turning and I took it. The road ahead looked clear.

"Dude, put your foot down," Mike said. "We want to get there before it gets dark."

"It's only two o clock, Mike."

"And you're doing ten miles an hour, Alex."

"If we see a checkpoint, I want to make sure I have time to stop before we crash into it and get caught."

"Let me drive."

"No, I'm driving."

"We'll never get to a boat at this rate."

"Mike," Lucy said, "Alex knows what he's doing."

I felt a sudden flush of pride. It was nice to have Lucy on my side.

Five minutes later, my strategy was proved right.

In the distance, I saw a dark bulky shape on the road. Slowing to a crawl, I pulled into the trees and killed the engine. "Looks like a checkpoint."

Mike turned to the girls. "Elena, pass the binoculars out of my rucksack."

She rummaged in the top pocket and handed him a small pair of binoculars encased in green rubber. He got out of the Land Rover and crept through the trees. Once he broke cover, he got onto his belly and crawled through the mud to the edge of the road.

He raised the binoculars to his eyes and studied the area along the road.

By the time he climbed back into the Land Rover, his jacket was smeared with mud and he had a worried look on his face.

"There's an armored personnel carrier on the road and six soldiers standing around it. There's a Land Rover as well but I couldn't see if there was anyone inside it."

I looked at the map. I couldn't see any way to get out of the mountains and to the coast without hitting a main road somewhere along the way. If all the roads were blocked like this, we were screwed.

I opened my door and got out, needing fresh air. The rain was letting up, slowing to an insidious drizzle and we were sheltered in the trees. Everyone got out of the Rover to stretch their legs. We were stuck here anyway. We couldn't go any further up the road without being spotted.

"Any ideas?" Mike said to no one in particular.

We were silent.

"Not unless we're willing to go on foot from here. But it's about forty miles to the coast and it isn't only the army we have to worry about." I didn't want to proceed on foot.

The Land Rover offered at least some protection. And there was no way we could hike forty miles before nightfall. I wasn't even sure I could hike forty miles at all.

Also, I didn't hold out much hope for our chances of survival without a vehicle. There must be thousands of zombies between here and the coast. We couldn't outrun them all.

The only other plan I could come up with involved driving around the roadblock. The Land Rover could handle the terrain by the side of the road but we couldn't exactly drive up the side of a mountain, which meant the soldiers would see us and start shooting. If we got past the bullets, they would probably chase us. I may be good at racing games on my consoles but in real life I didn't think I would manage to outrun solders in a high speed chase.

Lucy interrupted my thoughts. "Can you hear that?" She seemed to be listening to the forest.

"We need to get back in the Land Rover," I said. If there were zombies in the trees, I was getting us out of here.

"No, it's voices."

I listened. I heard it too. A lot of voices. Talking. The terrain sloped up steeply to a ridge. The sounds were coming from the other side.

"We should check it out, Man." Mike was already heading up the slope.

I looked at the girls and shrugged. There weren't any better options coming our way so we might as well see who was making all the noise. Maybe if it got louder, it would distract the soldiers at the checkpoint and we would be able to drive past unseen.

The slope steepened as we climbed and I had to hold on to pine tree trunks to prevent myself from slipping over on the carpet of pine needles on the ground.

When I finally got to the rocky ridge, I was out of breath and my lungs hurt.

"You won't believe this, Man." Mike stared down the slope on the other side, his eyes wide.

I looked over.

A wide area had been cleared in the trees and a settlement of green tents huddled together there. A wire fence surrounded the tent city and along the perimeter, wooden guard towers had been erected complete with search lights. There were four towers and each had two soldiers standing lookout by the searchlights. Soldiers patrolled the fence in pairs, some with dogs on leashes.

Inside the fence, civilians sat by the tents or paced the area between them. They looked miserable, as if they had lost all hope.

This was man's defence against the zombies.

A Survivors Camp.

Eight

I LOOKED DOWN AT THE misery and shuddered. What were the army hoping to achieve by caging up human beings like this? I had seen the broken fences at the farm and knew the wire surrounding the camp would be useless as protection against a zombie horde.

How long were they intending to keep people locked up like this? Even up here I could smell the camp's stink of human waste and fear. Lucy, Mike and Elena looked down at the scene with just as much horror as I felt.

"Maybe they have food down there," Elena said. Our supplies were low. We had only brought enough granola bars and packs of instant noodles to last us for two days of hiking and camping. The meal at the farmhouse had been a bonus but we had left so quickly that we didn't have time to grab food from the cupboards. Besides, Brand and

Cartwright would have known we were planning to escape if we stuffed our rucksacks with cans of beans.

"Maybe," I said, "but do we really want to go down there and find out?"

Mike pointed out a tent that had been erected outside the fence, near the trees. "I bet it's in there."

This was a bad idea. If we even tried to get down there we would get caught. I couldn't think of a worse way to spend the apocalypse than locked in a cage like cows in an abattoir.

Mike pulled us back from the rocks and looked at us solemnly. I knew that look. It meant Mike was trying to convey that what he was about to say was serious. "We can go down there, steal some food, and be gone before they even know it."

"This is crazy," I said. "There are going to be much easier places to get food than from a Survivors Camp. The place is crawling with soldiers."

"Why are they keeping people locked up like that?" Elena glanced back at the camp.

"They're trying to separate the infected from the uninfected. All they need to do is cage everyone up and see who turns. The ones who don't are clean." It sounded simple but even as I said it I realized that explanation didn't make sense. We had seen Cartwright turn in a matter of minutes. If the virus' incubation period was so short, all the people in the camp must be uninfected, otherwise they would have turned by now.

Unless the soldiers knew something we didn't.

66

"What about the food?" Mike looked eager to go down there.

"I'm not going," I said. "When we get to the coast, we can find an abandoned house and raid the pantry. We don't need to risk our lives like this."

"Alex is right," Lucy said.

"For fuck's sake, Alex is right," Mike mocked. "That's all I hear from you two… how right you are and how wrong I am. The Alex and Lucy mutual appreciation club."

"We *were* right about something going wrong with the world," she said calmly.

"Yeah, yeah, whatever. I'm coming up with a plan to get us some food…"

"It's a *bad* plan," I said.

He glared at me. "What do you know about plans, Alex? Unless it's a plan to storm an enemy castle in Warcraft, you don't know shit."

"Thanks for that, Mike. Well unless you haven't noticed, there's a fucking zombie apocalypse going on and I'm still alive."

"Only because you came away with me for the weekend."

"Really? I seem to remember it was me who got the keys to the Land Rover."

"Boys, please," Elena said, holding her arms up in a halting motion. "We'll all be dead if we keep arguing like this. We need to be quiet, remember?"

She was right. Not only were there soldiers around, there could be Nasties in these woods.

Mike dropped his voice to a whisper. "I'm just saying that we should consider going down there and getting some supplies."

"It's a bad idea, Man," I said, using the term of address he used all the time.

A growling erupted from the camp. That growl was neither human nor animal. I had heard that sound before, on the porch of the farmhouse. We clambered up to the rocks gain to get a better view.

The sound drifted from one of the tents. A painful growl. The people in the vicinity of the tent panicked, tried to run.

But there was nowhere to run.

A Nasty burst from the tent, grabbing the nearest victim it could find, a man in a neat black suit who looked almost surreally out of place in the camp, and bit his neck. Discarding his bleeding body, the zombie staggered toward a girl who looked like she could be maybe ten years old.

A woman in her thirties jumped forward between the girl and the zombie, telling the girl to run. Before the woman had a chance to take her own advice, the zombie had its teeth clamped around her shoulder.

A shot from outside the fence cracked the air.

The zombie's head burst open, black blood spewing from its pierced skull.

The woman screamed.

The monster fell heavily to the ground.

The man in the suit sat dazed, dabbing at the wound in his neck with a handkerchief.

Outside the fence, two soldiers unlocked the gate and stepped inside.

The little girl who had been saved rushed forward to the woman, crying. She flung her arms around her and buried her head against the woman's neck.

The soldiers reached the scene of the attack and one of them kicked the zombie's body, making sure it was dead.

The woman and girl sat hugging on the ground.

The suited man looked up as one of the soldier's approached him.

The second soldier walked over to the woman and girl. Pulled the girl away.

Dragged the woman to her feet.

She sobbed, looking at the girl. "My daughter!"

The little girl went to run forward to her mother. An older woman in the crowd held her back, her own eyes filling with tears.

The first soldier pulled the man in the suit up and led him into the tent the zombie had come from.

The second soldier followed, bringing the crying woman.

A moment of silence then two shots rang out from the tent.

The old woman clutched the little girl, letting her cry, rubbing her back to comfort her.

I turned away from the scene.

I didn't want to ever think again of what I had just seen but I knew it would haunt my nightmares for the rest of my life.

The sound of boots on the rocks to my left made me whirl around in that direction. A soldier stood over us, handgun pointed at me. He grinned humorlessly. "Don't even think about running."

He seemed to be alone, probably part of the checkpoint detail sent out to patrol the woods. He looked fresh and strong. The army were obviously looking after their own while the general population lived like caged animals. With his gun still trained on us, he unclipped a radio from his belt and brought it up to his mouth. "I've got four civvies up here. Over."

A static-filled reply, probably from the soldiers at the checkpoint, said, "OK, we'll be there in a minute. Over and out."

Mike cracked. I don't know if it was because of the scene we had just witnessed or because of the entire situation we found ourselves in but he leapt at the soldier.

Surprised, the soldier went down, Mike on top of him. They rolled down the slope, struggling against each other.

The gun went off.

A black cloud of starlings flocked from the trees at the sharp sound.

Mike and the soldier lay still.

I went down to see if my friend was still alive.

Slipped on the pine needles.

Slid to the two bodies.

Mike pushed himself away from the dead soldier. He picked up the pistol.

A dark blood stain covered the soldier's combat jacket.

I didn't care that a man was dead, I had seen what they were doing to the people in that camp. I only cared that my friend was alive.

Mike looked down at the dead body. He held the handgun loosely in his right hand.

The soldier's radio crackled from where it had been jammed beneath a tree root during the struggle. "Peterson, we heard a shot fired. Confirm. Over."

I grabbed it and switched it off. Stuffing it into my coat pocket, I put a hand on Mike's arm. "We need to go, Mike."

His eyes never left the dead soldier. "Yeah, Man."

Lucy appeared at my side. "There are more soldiers coming."

We could hear them coming through the woods below us, twigs cracking beneath their boots. If they found out we had killed one of their number, they might not even put us in the camp. A cold-blooded execution by the roadside was possible. In this society where the army kept citizens in cages and killed the bitten before they turned, what was to stop these soldiers killing us in cold blood? The fate of the girls might be even worse than that.

"We need to move," I said, vocalizing my thoughts. "This way. We can follow that stream down to the road and get to the Land Rover."

"Then what?" Lucy asked as we slipped and scrambled across the slope toward the stream that trickled down from the higher rocks.

"We have to go through the checkpoint. We don't have a choice now."

We climbed down carefully. The water gurgled over rocks and fallen branches in its unchanging course down the slope. Like this stream, society had forced its way constantly forward, cutting through barriers in its way until it got to the point it was at today. Perhaps the virus was inevitable, the result of what we had done to the planet, to other species, to our environment.

Maybe this was payback and all that lay at the end of our road forward was death. Unless survivors came out of this apocalypse unscathed, all that would be left of mankind would be a few shambling, rotting remnants.

How long would they last before they rotted away for good? The zombies would eventually die out just as humanity had and all that would be left of us would be dust.

The virus had chosen a host that was simply a collection of blood, bones, tissue and bacteria. The host would eventually rot and then the virus would be killed.

A memory entered my head but it meant nothing. It was something I had seen on TV once. A fish swimming in the shallows of a river being picked up by the hunting beak of a heron.

Why had that come to mind? I tried to remember more about the show but being chased by armed soldiers isn't conducive to remembering old TV programs.

We managed to get down the slope without breaking any bones and found the Land Rover. I climbed into the driver's seat and started the engine. The smell of petrol as the engine roared into life was comforting.

The girls climbed into the back and Mike slid into the passenger seat.

"Hit it, Man." His shock at killing the soldier seemed to be gone.

I slammed the gear stick into first and guided us out onto the road. In the rearview mirror, I saw two soldiers break from the trees. They dropped to a kneeling position, bringing up their rifles.

"Get down." I said, sliding down in my seat.

I tramped on the accelerator and got the Rover up into fourth gear as we sped along the road. Ahead, the dark bulk of the armored personnel carrier blocked the road. On the right, a green Land Rover was parked in the dirt. On the left was a small gap. Standing by the APC were three soldiers.

Judging by the surprised looks on their face, they hadn't been expecting a Land Rover to come speeding toward them.

Two of them threw cigarettes down onto the road. The butts sparked orange before dying.

Three thuds from the back of the vehicle told me we'd been hit. It sounded like the bullets tore into the back panel. I still had control of the wheel so at least they hadn't hit the tires.

The APC grew in the windscreen as I increased our speed.

The soldiers fumbled for their guns.

I wrenched the wheel and we left the road. The steering wheel shook in my hands as we hit undergrowth and uneven ground.

The dark green metal armor of the APC passed by my side window.

I pulled the wheel to the right and we slammed back onto the road.

In the rearview, I saw two of the soldiers running for their Land Rover.

They pulled onto the road behind us and the passenger leaned out of his window, aiming his assault rifle and spraying us with a hail of bullets.

We weren't going to make it to the coast.

Nine

"PUT YOUR FOOT DOWN!" MIKE shouted at me.

I had the accelerator pushed down to the floor. We were doing nearly a hundred miles an hour. The scenery flashed past the windows like a streaky oil painting. The sounds of shots from the soldier's gun were like exploding firecrackers. I looked in the rearview. They were gaining on us.

"Why don't you shoot back at them?" I said, indicating the gun on Mike's lap. "Try to hit a tire or something."

"Yeah, right. Like that's going to happen."

"Give me the gun," Lucy said from the back seat. "I'll do it."

He looked back at her. "You know how to shoot?"

"My dad's in a gun club. I go to the range with him all the time."

Mike looked as surprised. He passed the gun back to her.

I heard clicks as she checked the magazine and slid it home. "Colt M1911," she said. "Only five rounds left." Cold air rushed into the vehicle as she slid open the window and leaned out, facing backwards, gun raised.

She fired.

And missed.

"Stop moving all over the road," she demanded. "I need a steady shot."

I kept the wheel steady.

She fired again. In the rearview, the military Land Rover swerved.

Lucy came back in and closed the window. "You're going to have to outrun them, Alex. Shooting from a moving vehicle isn't as easy as it looks in the movies. We can't waste these bullets."

I nodded and kept the pedal to the floor.

The road twisted around the mountainous terrain and I had to hit the brakes at every bend, gearing down to take the turn before flooring the accelerator again. The soldier driving the chasing vehicle didn't seem to be any more familiar with these roads than I was. They dropped back on the tight turns and the distance between us and them increased.

I followed the road signs for Swansea, knowing I would have to take a different route to the coast once we got near the city because of the huge number of zombies that must be in that area.

I had no idea how we were going to be able to stop the Land Rover and find a boat before our pursuers either killed or caught us. That was something we would have to think about once we got to the sea.

Mike had the same thought. "What are we going to do when we have to stop, Man?"

"I don't know. We may have to run for a boat."

"This is a bad idea, Man."

"Any other suggestions?"

"I can't be put in one of those camps," Elena said.

After what we had seen, none of us wanted that.

The soldiers had stopped firing on us now, content to follow and wait. We couldn't outrun them forever.

Mike pointed at the road ahead. "There's another checkpoint, Man."

I saw the dark shape of the personnel carrier as soon as he said it. Maybe that was why our pursuers were staying back; they knew the soldiers at the checkpoint ahead would take us out.

Except there were no soldiers at the checkpoint ahead.

The APC sat alone and unattended.

As we got closer, I could see bodies strewn around the area. On the road, at the side of road and in the trees. Soldiers and zombies. The checkpoint had been attacked. The soldiers were dead.

I slowed down and drove around the personnel carrier. The road felt slippery beneath the tires and I tried not to think why. If it hadn't been for the soldiers driving behind us, we could have stopped and taken much-needed guns and supplies.

Although salvaging items from the carnage would have been a nightmare. Everywhere we looked, horror stared back at us. I kept my eyes fixed on the road ahead, trying to ignore the twisted and ripped bodies through my side window.The stench of guts and death drifted into the Land Rover as we drove past and made me feel like vomiting.

Crows perched atop the APC, ragged pieces of red flesh dangling from their black beaks.

We drove on and as soon as we got past the mess of bodies, I pressed the accelerator and didn't look in the rearview mirror until that place of death was out of sight.

Then I checked the mirror several times, The road behind was empty.

"The soldiers aren't following us anymore."

Mike looked over his shoulder. "Maybe seeing their dead friends spooked them."

I wasn't so sure. It didn't feel right that they were letting us go.

"That was unreal, Man. We need to get on a boat and leave this shit behind."

Mike seemed to think that a boat would solve all our problems. It would solve some of them. We would be able to sleep safely at night. We could spend days out on the sea, away from the zombies. But we still needed to eat. There would be food runs, during which we would have to land the boat, or at least row to shore and raid the houses, villages and towns along the coast. We couldn't 'leave this shit behind', we could only try to survive it.

I didn't say anything to Mike. No need to slap him around the face with a cold dose of reality. He had been through enough today. We all had. I envied his ability to dream of an escape, to actually think life could be good again.

It was a probably a result of his life experience so far. Mike had it easy. He was good-looking, physical, charming. He might not be the sharpest tool in the box but he was a man's man. His poor school grades were the gateway through which we met. I helped him do a Math assignment at school. At the time, I did it because I thought Mike was going to beat me up if I didn't. Later, we discovered that despite our social differences, we shared some interests. Mike liked to play video games when he wasn't playing sports and once he saw my collection of titles, he realized I wasn't just a game player, I was a game geek.

I introduced him to the online worlds and therefore also to my world. In return, he invited me to events that were outside of my comfort zone. He didn't care what his friends, mainly jocks, said about him bringing a geek to parties. As far as Mike was concerned, we were friends and that was that.

He was good like that.

If it wasn't for Mike, I wouldn't be alive now.

I would never have gone to Doug Latimer's barbecue. That led to coming to Wales in a desperate attempt to speak to Lucy Hoffmeister. If I had stayed at home, I would most likely be dead. I owed Mike my life.

So instead of saying, 'No, Mike, we are never going to leave this shit behind. Even if we get a boat we are still going to be in the shit because we have needs like every human being and if those needs aren't met, we die,' I looked across at him and gave him a thin-lipped smile.

"Don't worry, Mike, we'll get a boat."

But first we had to get to the coast. I couldn't understand why the soldiers had stopped chasing us. If they had friends at that checkpoint, why not chase us down and come back later? It wasn't like any of those soldiers were going anywhere.

Or was that it? Had they stopped to make sure their friends *weren't* going anywhere? The bodies had been in pieces but that didn't mean some of them couldn't be in a zombie state. The two soldiers had probably pulled over to deliver head shots to any infected.

That gave us a chance to get away.

"Mike, look out!"

Lucy's voice brought me snapping back to reality. Ahead on the road, two cars lay across both lanes. It looked like they had plowed into each other at high speed. The bodywork was mostly wrecked. Carpets of glass lay twinkling in the sunlight all across the road. I couldn't see any survivors. There was no way around the wreckage.

Unless we moved it quickly, we were trapped.

Ten

I STOPPED THE LAND ROVER but kept the engine running. As soon as I got out, I could smell petrol and burned flesh. A white Ford Focus lay on its side across the road. Its tail was facing us so I couldn't see if there was anyone inside. A dark blue Chrysler Cruiser sat on its wheels but its front was destroyed, the engine sticking up through a gash in the bodywork like an erupted boil.

The air bags had inflated so we couldn't see the driver.

I leaned into the Land Rover. "Lucy, hand me the gun."

She passed it to me. "The safeties are off," she said. "Be careful."

I nodded. "Keep an eye on the road behind us in case those soldiers show up."

Holding the gun in my right hand, muzzle pointed to the ground, I strode across to the crash site. Mike joined me, brandishing a large branch he had found at the roadside. I hoped his clubbing would be more accurate than my shooting. I had never fired a real gun in my life.

We approached the Focus first. As soon as we got close, the smell of death became overwhelming. Mike grabbed my arm. "There's no one alive in there, Man."

He was right. There had once been a family of four in that car. Now, every inch of unbroken glass was tinted red with blood. Through the broken windows we could see the bodies. Still buckled in by their seat belts. All of them had turned. They glared at us with their yellow eyes and began to emit that eerie moan of hunger.

We stepped back instinctively even though they were trapped in there. I wondered if they had been infection-free when they crashed. Maybe the same zombies that had killed the checkpoint soldiers had come upon this family in the overturned car and gone to work on them. Or maybe the family had simply died in the crash and then turned because everybody turns after death. That was how it worked in all of George A. Romero's movies, anyway, as well as in a few TV shows.

But the air bags were inflated so I assumed it wasn't the crash that had killed them, it was roaming zombies.

We moved away and went to the Cruiser. The driver was dead. And human. His face rested on the air bag as if he were simply lying on a pillow. He was in his fifties, balding, and wearing glasses that were still intact. There was no blood, no wounds. What had killed him? A heart attack?

On the passenger seat, a road atlas lay open. The hospital in Brecon was circled in red pen.

A sudden movement from the back seat surprised us. I raised the pistol automatically, peering through the window.

A grey-haired woman sat on the backseat, dressed in a white nightgown and green bath robe. She had turned. Struggling against the seat belt that held her in place, she gnashed her teeth at us and growled.

"Fuck," Mike said.

"Looks like he was taking his wife to hospital and she turned in the back seat. He had a heart attack and crashed into the Focus. They got turned before they got out of the car. There must have been zombies in the area."

"So why didn't they turn him? He looks normal."

"He was already dead. The virus wants to spread itself. There's no point infecting someone who isn't going anywhere."

Mike nodded at the Focus. "They aren't going anywhere either."

"But they were alive so the virus could infect them, kill them and raise them from the dead. Now they have the potential to spread it by killing others." I looked at the way the cars were blocking the road. If we could move the Cruiser, we should be able to make it past the Focus. "We need to see if there's a tow rope in the Land Rover."

We walked back to our vehicle and opened the back. A length of thick blue rope lay amongst various tools and a tire iron. Mike took the rope while I turned the Land Rover around so the back faced the Cruiser.

"Are there any survivors?" Elena asked as I performed the manoeuvre.

"No," I said. "Everyone's dead."

I got out and Mike tied one end of the rope to the tow bar on the Rover. I found a piece of solid chassis on the Cruiser and tied the rope to it. Getting back in the Rover, I put it into first and slowly let up the clutch. The vehicle moved forward until the rope tautened. Then I gave it more gas gradually until it moved forward again, slower this time as it pulled the weight of the Cruiser.

I drove forward twenty feet, creating enough of a gap to get our vehicle through.

As I stopped and put the Rover into neutral, I told Mike to untie the rope.

"We need to move fast," he said, pointing at the woods near the Focus.

There must have been twenty of them coming through the trees, lumbering toward the road. Maybe they were the group that had turned the family in the car. Our noise had attracted them and now they wanted our blood.

Mike went to work on the rope, untying it from the Rover. He went to the Cruiser but I stopped him. "Leave it, Mike. We don't have time." I waited for him to get back in the Land rover before I turned it so we were facing the right way. The zombies were all over the road, staggering toward us.

"Go, Man!"

I stamped on the accelerator and we lurched forward into them. A Nasty that had once been a young woman with long blonde hair went down under the front bumper. We drove over her and Rover shuddered as her bones broke beneath the wheels.

Hands grabbed at our vehicle, sliding greasily along the windows as we drove past. Yellow eyes set in blue mottled faces stared in at us with hatred and hunger.

We got past them and I let out a breath of relief.

"If those soldiers are still following us, they'll get a nasty surprise," Lucy said.

I frowned. It was still worrying me that the soldiers had given up. We had spent long enough at the crash site for them to catch up with us if they were still coming this way. Maybe they had just been low on fuel and had turned back. No, they wouldn't have a vehicle parked at a check point with no petrol in the tank. It didn't make sense.

"Mike," I said, "check that map. Back where that last checkpoint was, I thought I saw a side road. Where does it lead?"

He picked up the map and traced back along the road we were on with his finger. "Yeah, it's here. It cuts through some farmland and a couple of villages."

"Does it meet up with this road again?"

He scanned the map and nodded. "Yeah, near the coast. There's a crossroads. That road meets up with this one."

They were going to cut us off.

I told the others. The soldiers were waiting for us ahead.

According to the road signs, we were only a couple of miles from the coast. At a speed of sixty miles an hour, which was the speed we were travelling at, we would be there in two minutes. Straight into an ambush.

There was no going back now. We had to get to a boat before nightfall. We needed safety, a place to sleep. These woods were dangerous. This area was crawling with zombies and soldiers. We had to take our chances at the coast. To stay here would mean death.

I increased our speed to eighty and peered at the road ahead. The rain started again and I put the wipers on at full speed. The sound of the blades wiping rhythmically across the wet glass was like a countdown, ticking off the seconds until we reached the crossroads.

Daylight was fading and my hope seemed to be going with it. Were these our last moments? I couldn't accept that. I pressed the accelerator and the speedometer needle climbed up to ninety.

"There they are, Man." Mike pointed at the crossroads ahead. The army Land Rover was parked on the side road, headlights cutting through the evening gloom. Positioned next to the vehicle were the two soldiers. They saw us coming and adopted firing positions.

"Where do the roads go?" I asked Mike frantically.

"This road heads down to a marina. The side roads just go along the top of the cliffs."

We had to get to the marina. If the Land Rover could withstand the bullets they were about to spray us with, we might be able to get to the marina and onto a boat before they got back into their vehicle and caught up with us.

We were almost at the crossroads.

"Hold on," I said.

The firing started.

Bullets peppered the Land Rover and I heard both tires blow out. The steering wheel juddered in my hand. I lost control.

We careened off the road and onto grass.

I fought with the wheel.

Elena screamed from the back seat.

I saw the grass disappear ahead. Disappear into darkness. The cliff edge.

The ground beneath the flat tires was rough, bumpy.

Then suddenly it was gone.

We were in the air, flipping and falling.

The rocky wall of the cliff hurtled by the windows. Below us the dark churning sea waited.

We hit the water like it was a concrete wall and everything went black.

Eleven

"ALEX!"

The voice came from far away. I felt hands on my shoulders, shaking me. Something very cold covered my legs. Wet and cold.

I opened my eyes. We were sinking. Waves lashed against the windows. Freezing water poured in over our legs. "Is everyone OK?" I asked.

"As good as we can be in the situation," Mike said. "Alex, we're sinking."

I nodded, trying to clear my vision of the black floating spots that danced there. "We can't open the doors until the car fills with water. Something about equalizing pressure."

"We'll fucking freeze to death by then, Man!"

"So we need to break the windscreen and climb out."

Mike looked around for something to break the glass. "The tire iron," he said. "Elena, it's in the back."

She leaned over the back seat and into the trunk. She grabbed the tire iron and handed it to Mike.

The sea water was rising. It spread over the seats.

Mike took a swing at the windscreen and managed to crack it. A second blow shattered the safety glass. We both used our legs to push it clear of the frame.

"Bring the rucksacks," Mike said. "There are things in there we'll need."

The girls passed the rucksacks forward.

"Tie the straps together," I suggested. "They'll float. We won't lose them if they're all tied together."

Mike unfastened the clips and attached the straps so the rucksacks were looped together. He pushed them out through the hole where the windscreen had been and climbed out onto the hood. I followed him and we helped the girls clamber through.

With our weight on top of it, the Land Rover sank quickly into the deep water.

"See that beach," Mike said, pointing at a stretch of sand beneath the cliffs. "Head for that." He pushed the rucksack raft into the water and followed it. I let myself fall forward into the water and gasped as I felt the icy wetness cover my body. I grabbed the rucksacks and kicked my legs to stay afloat.

The four of us used the raft to stay together, each of us holding onto the slippery fabric and swimming toward the beach.

I glanced back to where the Land Rover had been. It was gone, buried beneath the waves.

I spat out a salty mouthful of cold seawater and scanned the beach. It appeared deserted. As darkness fell, so did the rain, fat drops splashing into the water around us. I looked up at the cliffs where we had gone over the edge. It must be at least a fifty foot drop. We were lucky to be alive.

I felt something grasp my legs and I cried out, certain that a zombie was standing down there under the water and had curled his rotting hands around my calf.

"It's just weeds," Mike said, his teeth chattering with cold.

I looked at Lucy. Her lips were turning blue and her skin was pale, making her appear like a beautiful vampire.

We reached the shallows and stood up, dragging the rucksacks out of the water.

"What now?" I asked.

Mike looked along the cliff wall. "There must be caves. There are always caves."

That was true. I remembered many family holidays when I was a kid, exploring caves along the beach with Joe while Mom and Dad sat on sun loungers. There were always caves.

We set off along the wet sand. The rain lashed into our faces, making it hard to see. I put my hand up to ward it off but I had to keep blinking raindrops from my eyes. It made it harder to find a cave. Worse, I was afraid we wouldn't be able to see the zombies. There would be nothing more tragic than surviving this far only to stumble into a zombie in the rain.

"There's a cave," Lucy shouted, pointing to the rocks with a trembling hand.

A dark gap in the cliff wall led into darkness.

We made for it, shuffling through the sand until we stood at the mouth of the cave. Mike searched through the side pocket of his rucksack and got a flashlight. He shone the beam into the blackness. Shadows fled to the edges of the space he illuminated.

The sand on the floor in there was dry. The space was big enough for all of us to fit inside. We got in out of the rain and Mike lit the kerosene lamps, placing them at the back of the cave so the light wouldn't spill out onto the beach outside.

There was driftwood in here. It looked like someone visited this cave regularly and built fires here. Before the world went to hell. Blackened and charred wood lay in the center of a circle of stones. I placed fresh wood in there and Mike lit it. As the fire sparked into life, we huddled around it, removing our soaked jackets and laying them on the sand by the rocky wall.

"I'm going to get changed," Elena said, digging into her rucksack.

"So am I," Lucy agreed.

They fished out dry clothes and stood in the heat of the fire. I watched as they peeled off their wet clothing. Mike looked a me and grinned then stared at the girls, firelight glowing in his eyes.

As they stripped down to their underwear, I felt myself getting excited despite the cold, wet cargo pants clinging to me. Elena was much thinner than Lucy, her ribs showing beneath her black bra. Her legs were sleek and muscled.

Lucy's curves made her appear more womanly in my eyes. Her breasts thrust against her pink bra, her cleavage deep between the swells of soft flesh. Her waist was small above the inviting curves of her hips. Her pink panties were small too and when she turned around to protect her modesty while she removed her bra, the firelight cast flickering shadows over the smooth slopes of her buttocks.

She removed the panties and quickly replaced them with a fresh, dry pair. White with tiny blue flowers printed on the cotton. She put on a matching bra before slipping on a black t-shirt and blue jeans.

When the girls turned to face us, we were sitting there with huge grins on our faces.

Elena looked at Lucy and raised an eyebrow. "Looks like the boys are happy about something."

We all laughed. It was a moment of light relief in an otherwise shitty day.

"It's your turn now, boys," Elena said.

I looked at Mike and he shrugged. We did need to get out of our wet things. I found my dry clothes and faced away from the girls while I stripped. Mike did the same except he spun around for a split second to give the girls a flash of his goods. I remained as hidden as I could in the shadows. Working a sedentary job and playing video games is not the way to get a great physique.

I hurried into my clothes and returned to warm myself by the fire as quickly as I could.

Lucy looked into my eyes. "You've got nothing to be embarrassed about."

I was thankful she didn't know the non-history of my non-existent love life. Apart from the prostitute in Amsterdam, my only other experience in the sex department had been with a girl named Gina Lewis when I was twenty-one. Gina was as much of a geek as I was and we met in Second Life one afternoon when I was off sick from work. I actually only had a cold but I rang in and said I had the flu because I wanted a couple of days off to stay in bed and play on the computer. I took enough shit at work to have a couple extra days off at my discretion.

On this particular sunny afternoon, I was propped up against the pillows balancing the laptop on my knee when I ran into Gina. We had a chat and it turned out she lived in Manchester, which was only an hour's drive from my house.

Gina was online looking for a man. As obsessed with games as I was but without a Mike equivalent to get her out of the house, she lived most of her life online. She worked freelance, writing manuals for software companies, so she didn't even have contact with work colleagues. Every now and then she craved human contact so she went online to find a man who lived close by.

And so I had spent an hour driving to Manchester followed by an hour of sex. I didn't see Gina again and she never contacted me.

So I reckoned my embarrassment in front of Lucy was justified.

I stared into the fire and let it warm my face.

I felt exhausted. Today had been the longest day of my life. I had experienced every emotion possible and almost been killed a number of times. "Someone should be on guard duty," I said. "We can take turns."

We arranged a shift pattern which meant I had two hours sleep before it was my turn to keep watch for an hour. Laying the sleeping bags out in the sand, we agreed that the guard would have the gun.

I put my head down and closed my eyes. The soft sand shifted beneath my sleeping bag, adjusting to my body. This was more comfortable than the ground on the mountain. I fell asleep almost immediately.

And dreamed of a fish swimming in the shallows before being picked up by a heron and eaten.

Twelve

I KNEW WHAT THE DREAM meant. I sat by the entrance of the cave on my guard shift, watching the rain pour down over the sea and sand and cliffs, and I knew why I had dreamed of the fish and the heron.

It was because of the virus.

I had seen a TV show once about how viruses controlled the hosts they infected. There was a virus that infected insects then made them climb as high as they could up a plant or a tree so the virus could send out spores to infect more insects. The higher the spores were, the better they could catch the breeze and travel further.

The virus that infected the fish I had dreamed about was a waterborne virus that wanted to infect birds, not fish at all. But it started in rivers because it was spread in bird faeces. So it infected a fish host then made that host swim in the shallows in a manner that would attract hungry birds. The birds ate the fish and became infected. The virus got to where it wanted to be.

So now there was a virus infecting everyone and my mind had looked back in its data banks for any information it had about viruses and brought up memories of that TV show. Interesting but useless to me in my current situation.

If a virus could control its host like that, it explained why the zombies were seeking out prey. The virus wanted to spread. But we already guessed that so nothing new there. Thanks, brain, but you're on the the wrong track. An old TV show about ants and fish isn't really relevant in a zombie apocalypse.

I was bored and hungry. Tomorrow we needed to find a boat and food. As for boredom, staring at a rainy beach for an hour was mind numbing. I unzipped the pocket on my jacket and took out the army radio we had taken from the soldier. It looked and felt dry. The hiking jacket had waterproof pockets but I didn't think that included being immersed in the sea so I was surprised that the radio seemed to be intact.

I clicked it on. Static came out of the speaker. I turned the volume down and found the tuning dial. With the radio to my ear, I searched for a signal. Maybe I could pick up a conversation between soldiers in the area.

I thought I caught a snatch of a word for a second but it got lost in all the hissing static. Maybe the water had affected the radio after all. I turned the dial the opposite direction slowly, scanning back across the channels.

"…That's what I think anyway. Over."

My fingers froze on the dial.

"Yeah, I know but we have to follow orders, Jim. These things are decided at a much higher pay grade than ours, Mate. Over."

"The fucking U.N. Who put them in charge? And why do they get to come sailing in on their fucking rescue mission and get all the fucking glory when it's us who've done all the grunt work? Have they been separating the uninfected from the zombies? Have they fuck. We run all the risks and they come in for the medals. It pisses me off. Over."

"Relax. It'll all be done soon. Over."

"It'll be done alright. Done and dusted. Do you know what they're going to do to this country once they get the uninfected out? I heard they're going to nuke it. Nuke Britain. What gives them the right to do that to our country? Over."

"That's just a rumor, Jim. Don't go spreading it around. Anyway, once we're gone, there will only be Nasties left so why not nuke the place? Over."

"Because it's…oh fuck, I've got to go. The Captain is coming this way. Over and out."

I sat staring at the green military radio in my hand, trying to process what I had just heard. The U.N. were staging a rescue mission and then they were going to launch a nuclear strike on the zombies. That meant the entire world wasn't affected by the apocalypse. If the U.N. were still operating, they must have a base somewhere. If they were rescuing survivors, they must have somewhere to take them.

That explained the Survivor Camps. The British Army had been instructed to separate the uninfected in preparation for a rescue mission. The soldier on the radio said the U.N. were going to come 'sailing in' so that probably meant they were coming here on ships.

I scanned the other radio channels, desperate for more information, but all I got was static.

When I woke Elena for her shift, I told her to try the radio every now and then to see if she could pick up any more military chatter. She nodded wearily and took her post by the cave entrance while I crawled back into my sleeping bag.

I lay looking up at the darkness for awhile before I could get to sleep. There was a way out of all this. We just needed to find out where and when the U.N. ships were going to land. Maybe Joe and my parents would be rescued too. If they had been taken to a Survivors Camp and avoided infection, they could be among the ones waiting to be rescued.

The chance of that was slim. I knew that but still my spirits were lifted. We just had to make it to those ships. Maybe Mike had been right to be optimistic earlier and there *was* a a way to escape all of this.

I closed my eyes and dared to dream.

But my dream wasn't about rescue ships or Joe or my parents. I stood on the beach outside the cave. The sky was clear and the sun shone bright. The beach was deserted, the golden sand stretching off into the distance, but I didn't mind having the place to myself. This was a good day to be at the beach. I raised my face to the sun and felt its warmth bathe my skin.

Movement in the sea caught my eye and I looked out to where two shapes were rising from the waves. One dark-haired, one blonde. Both naked. Elena and Lucy. They waded in toward the beach, their long hair covering their faces. As they got closer, I could see their breasts; Elena's small and perky, Lucy's rounded and full. I got a sudden erection and realized I was naked too.

The girls were in the shallows now, the sea water lapping against their thighs. They stopped there and I knew they wanted me. Their need pulsed from them like a thick, heady scent.

I went to them, running over the hot sand until I was ankle-deep in the warm sea.

Both girls looked up, the hair falling back from their faces.

They glared at me with their hateful yellow eyes.

* * *

I sat up, immediately awake and disoriented. Where was I? The rock walls felt like they were closing in on me. The cave. I was in the cave. It was just a dream. A nightmare.

I lay back down and glanced over at the cave entrance. Lucy sat there, gun in hand, army radio on the sand by her feet. She leaned back against the rock, watching the rain hiss down over the sand outside.

"It's still raining," she said, looking over at me.

"Typical Welsh weather."

She nodded. "I didn't pick anything up on the radio."

I sat up and rubbed my eyes. We had kept the fire burning all night and I had slept in my clothes so despite the weather I felt warm and dry. "We need to find out where those U.N. ships are going to land." We had relayed the information I picked up from the radio during the night. Now all of us were hoping to be rescued.

"We'll keep checking." She stood up and stretched, those perfect breasts I had first seen at Doug Latimer's house pressing against the fabric of her t-shirt. She waved me over. "Look at this." She pointed out along the coastline.

I squinted into the rain. "What am I looking at?"

"About three miles along the beach. Just offshore."

I saw a white shape but it was too far to distinguish any details. "What is it?"

"I think it's a boat. It's been there all night."

I delved into Mike's rucksack and brought out the binoculars. It was a boat. A long white yacht. The type of pleasure craft wealthy people spend their summers on, cruising the Riviera or the Bahamas. I concentrated the binoculars on the windows. No movement inside that I could see. Painted in blue script on the white hull was the name The Big Easy. I hoped the name was prophetic.

"Looks like it's anchored there." I handed Lucy the binoculars.

She took a look and nodded. "So how do we get out to it?"

"There must be a rowboat or something around here somewhere. There's a marina just along the coast." I didn't want to go to the marina if we could avoid it. It was situated in the city, which meant zombies. A lot of zombies.

That boat, anchored tantalisingly close to the shore, seemed like our best option to remain safe while we tried to figure out the U.N. rescue plan. I judged the distance from the shoreline to the boat to be maybe half a mile. We could cover that distance in a rowboat in a short time and be in a zombie-free environment. We still needed food but we could sail along the coast and find a house or a village to raid.

I hoped it was going to be that easy. The beach was eerily quiet except for the constant sound of the sea breaking on the pebbles and the rain hitting the rocks. It seemed *too* quiet. We weren't all that far from Swansea, a city with a population of two hundred and forty thousand people before the virus outbreak. There should be more zombies around. I didn't believe the military had eradicated that many of them.

I kept my thoughts to myself. I wasn't about to complain out loud about the lack of zombies. If it meant we could get to The Big Easy without much trouble, that suited me just fine.

I didn't want to look into a pair of yellow eyes again for as long as I lived.

Thirteen

W E PACKED UP OUR STUFF and hoisted the rucksacks onto our backs. Lucy had the gun in case we met anyone along the beach but the area looked deserted. Mike led the way, striding along the wet sand as if he were out for a pleasant walk along the seashore. Elena kept up with him while Lucy and I trailed behind. This was now the accepted formation of our group and one that we fell into easily. I liked it for two reasons. One: I didn't have to keep up with Mike and Elena and two: I could talk with Lucy.

"Where do you think the U.N. are going to take the survivors?" she said as we walked beneath the cliffs.

"I don't know. America maybe. We don't know which countries have been affected and which ones are virus-free. If the U.S. closed down their borders as soon as they heard about the outbreak in India and Britain, it's possible they could be uncontaminated. Or maybe somewhere in Europe like France or Spain."

"If those places are clean, we could just sail there ourselves on the boat," she said.

"We could but if the U.N. has sanctioned a rescue operation, I would say only their ships would be allowed to dock anywhere. A small boat trying to do the same would probably get shot out of the water by the coastguard of whatever country it tried to dock in. If some countries are uninfected, they'll be doing everything in their power to stay that way."

"Yeah, I guess so."

"So unless we get onboard one of the U.N. ships, we're stuck." The problem with getting onto one of the rescue ships, we knew, was that we hadn't been part of the military 'cleansing' operation. We hadn't been certified uninfected in the Survivors Camps. We were going to have to try and sneak on board a U.N. ship.

"Do you really think they'll nuke Britain?" Lucy asked.

"I don't know. The soldier said that was just a rumor but it makes sense. Once they've saved everyone they're going to save, why not just nuke the rest? They're dead anyway. The survivors still left in the country won't last all that long."

"It seems extreme. The nuclear fallout will cause problems to the uninfected countries as well as Britain."

"They're trying to eradicate the virus from the planet. They'll have to pay a price to do that. They're probably willing to pay that price if it means future generations can live in a world without the zombie virus."

It did seem extreme but the countries that were zombie-free wanted to remain that way. If that meant a final solution involving nuclear warheads, then so be it. The future of the world was at stake here. Nobody cared about the individuals fighting to survive the armageddon on a day by day basis. The politicians and the military would look at this situation on a worldwide scale. Even killing a million innocent citizens could be justified if it meant the survival of the planet.

Mike and Elena stopped up ahead. Lying on the sand was an upturned rowboat, its mooring rope tied around a large rock to keep it from drifting out to sea. Mike flipped it over and stood by it, grinning. "We can get out of here, Man."

The little boat looked like it was used for fishing. Nets and lobster traps lay in the sand next to where it was tied. The oars were inside, attached by hooks to the wooden slats.

This little wooden craft had once been someone's livelihood. That person was probably dead now but his boat was going to give us a slim chance to live.

* * *

We reached the Big Easy half an hour later, approaching the large yacht from the stern. Mike was on the oars. Elena sat at the back of the rowboat while Lucy and I sat at the front. Lucy had the gun ready in her hand in case the boat was occupied.

We weren't going to kill anyone onboard if they were living people. In that case, we would leave them be and row away to find another boat. If the occupants of the Big Easy were undead though, we needed to be prepared.

Mike guided to rowboat to the rear of the yacht where a metal-runged ladder was affixed to the stern. I grabbed the cold metal to hold us steady while Lucy and Mike climbed up to the deck. I waited nervously, expecting to hear a gunshot or a scream but everything was quiet. Mike's head appeared, a grin on his face.

"It's all clear."

Elena climbed up and I followed after throwing up the rowboat's mooring line for Mike to tie it to a cleat on the yacht's stern.

The Big Easy was large enough to live on. We stood an an aft deck which had a small cockpit and cushioned seats. A wooden door opened into a living area which contained a small kitchen complete with refrigerator and a dining table. A door to the bow opened onto a sunbathing deck.

"The bedrooms and toilet are below," Mike said. "Everything we need."

I went back outside to the cockpit and looked at the wheel and throttle. "We have a problem," I said.

Mike poked his head through the door. "What is it, Man?"

"No keys to start the engine."

He pointed up a ladder. "The bridge is up there. I'm betting there's a spare pair of keys hidden away somewhere." He climbed the ladder and a few minutes later I heard the engine turn over then kick into life. Mike shouted down, "Got it!"

I climbed up to the bridge. Mike was inspecting the dials and gauges on the instrument panel. "Looks like this boat was used for cruising and fishing. There's a FishFinder on here. And there's fishing gear in the hold. We can fish for our food, Man."

It sounded perfect. That was what worried me. My motto had always been that if something seemed too good to be true, it probably was.

"How are we for fuel?"

He looked at the gauges. "Low. Very low."

My motto proved itself correct yet again.

I looked out through the window and along the coast. What I was about to suggest filled me with dread. "I suppose we'll have to go to the marina and fill the tank."

He looked at me and the smile that had been on his face a second ago vanished. "I suppose we will."

"I don't like the idea any more than you do," I said, "but we need the fuel. Otherwise we're stuck here floating near the shore. We'd be much safer if we sailed out into deeper waters."

He nodded, looking through the rain-streaked window at the shoreline. We were too visible here. The army could see us easily, might even be able to hit us with mortars fired from the cliffs. We weren't out of danger yet. But with a single run to the marina, we could set ourselves up for a long time, at least for as long as we had to wait for the U.N. rescue ships to arrive. There would be stores there. A moment of risk now would take away such risk in the near future. Once we were refuelled and stocked with supplies, we could sail out into open water.

We had nothing to lose. If we arrived at the marina and found it overrun with zombies, we could move on and come back later. From the Big Easy, we could check the place out from the safety of the sea.

Mike found a map of the coastline and located the marina. While he learned the yacht controls, I went back down to the aft deck and made sure the rowboat was securely tied. A clanking, winding sound told me Mike had found the controls to pull up the anchor. The engine revved a little and we moved forward slowly, our nose pointing up along the shoreline.

As we made our way past the beach, I unhooked a hand axe from where it hung next to a fire extinguisher and I swung it in the air a few times, as if attacking an imaginary opponent.

I wanted to be ready for whatever awaited us at the marina.

Fourteen

WHEN THE CITY OF SWANSEA appeared off the bow, I squinted against the falling rain at the buildings and streets visible from the sea. Mike had taken us out into deeper waters as a precaution and the rain made it harder to see anything clearly but the city looked deathly quiet.

Something wasn't right. The city shouldn't be like this. I had expected to see zombies lumbering around the streets. The city should be full of the hungry groans of the undead.

This unearthly silence chilled me to the bone.

Mike shouted down from the bridge. "You see that, Man? It's too good to be true."

Those were my thoughts exactly. I remembered the zombies at the farmhouse and how they had waited silently on the porch until we came out of the house. I didn't think they had the reasoning power to set such a trap but now, as I looked at the ghostly city in the rain, I wondered if we were heading straight into an ambush.

The rain bothered me. I went through the door into the living room.

The girls were in the kitchen, sorting through the cupboards and making a list of what food we had and what we needed. Because this boat was used for long trips, the cupboard contained long life products, mainly in cans, so it was perfect for our needs.

I wiped rainwater from my face and peered through the window at the tall buildings and empty coastline. I still had the axe gripped in my right hand.

"What's up, Alex?" Lucy asked from the counter where she and Elena had piled up packets of rice and cans of beans.

"It's just so quiet. Where are all the people who lived here? Where are all the zombies?"

"He's complaining because there *aren't* zombies?" Elena asked, rolling her eyes. "You really are weird, Alex."

Weird or not, I still couldn't shake my feeling of unease.

A speaker set into the wall crackled and Mike's voice came out of it. "Hey, can you guys hear me? I can see the marina."

I went out and up the ladder to the bridge.

Mike was bringing us in closer to the shore. Ahead, the twin jetties of the marina jutted out into the sea. There were boats everywhere. Most were moored in the slips but some floated freely on the tide. "I don't get it, Man," Mike said, "why didn't everybody just take the boats when they knew about the zombies?"

"The virus spread fast. By the time people knew what was happening, the army was probably rounding them up for the Survivors Camps."

There no people on the jetties, no sign of life. No sign of the undead.

Mike brought us around so we faced the docks. There were two fuel pumps, one at either side of the marina. We sailed toward the closest one and I jumped off the Big Easy onto the jetty, mooring rope in hand. Before I tied the boat to one of the steel cleats, I listened to the marina. All I could hear was rain bouncing off the boats and splashing into the water. I tied a fast and loose knot in case we had to leave here quickly.

Mike jumped up onto the dock and inspected the pump. "Looks like someone left it switched on. So at least some people got away on boats."

I looked toward the marine supply shop on shore. It looked quiet enough. "How long will it take to fill the tank?" I asked Mike.

"About ten minutes."

Climbing back onto the Big Easy, I grabbed the gun from where Lucy had left it on the dining table and headed back outside.

"Where you going?" Lucy asked.

"There's a store here. I'm going to check it out."

"Want me to come with?"

"No, it looks deserted."

Elena looked up from the piles of food they had arranged across every available kitchen surface. "We need sugar if they have any."

"I'll see what I can do."

I grabbed the binoculars, climbed back out onto the dock and looked toward the marine supply store through the magnifying lenses. A glass door gave me a view into the shop. A second door on the far side of the building led to the street beyond. That didn't make me happy. There were two ways into the shop which meant zombies could come in off the street. I couldn't see that street from where I stood so I decided to check everything out and lock the street door, if it wasn't already locked, before I salvaged supplies from the store.

With the gun in one hand and the axe in the other, I walked along the wooden dock.

A large poster inside the shop window had a picture of a man and woman drinking champagne on the back of a luxury yacht with the slogan 'Sail To Your Destiny'. The world that poster belonged to no longer existed.

I glanced into each moored boat as I passed, looking for movement inside. Nothing. The boats sat silently waiting for owners who would never return. For most of these craft, this was the end of the line. Unless other survivors found them, they would float here until they rotted into the sea.

I reached the shop door and looked through the glass. It was dark inside but I could make out racks of clothing, fishing gear, a bookshelf crammed with books, and shelves of food. No movement. No sounds from within.

I slid the axe into the leg pocket of my cargo pants and put my hand on the cold, wet metal door handle. Holding my breath, I gently pulled the door open. Nothing jumped out at me. No yellow eyes appeared in the shadows. I sniffed the air inside. No rank decaying meat smell assaulted my nostrils.

I slipped inside.

Stood by the half open door.

Listened.

The gun felt slippery in my hand.

No sound except the rain outside and the whirr of the pump at the end of the dock as Mike refuelled our boat.

I took two steps into the shop, my wet boots squeaking on the floor.

The clothing racks cast deep shadows over some areas of the room. I wished I could see if anything was hiding in those shadows.

The door and windows looking out onto the street showed me a deserted road lined with more shops. There was nobody out there. I crossed the room quickly, arcing the gun in front of me in case anything jumped out at me. The door to the street was unlocked and without a key I had no way of changing that situation. I went to the counter where a display of GPS units in a glass case stared at me with blank screens. Hopping over the counter I looked for a light switch. When I found it on the wall behind the cash register, I debated whether I should use it.

First of all, I didn't even know if there was electricity still running to the shop. Secondly, switching on the lights would give away my position to anyone out there in the street. Just because I couldn't see anybody didn't mean there wasn't someone out there somewhere. That thought chilled me.

Leaving the switch alone, I went back into the main part of the store and found a rank of small metal shopping carts lined up near the door. Wheeling one over to the clothing racks, I filled it with t-shirts, sweaters, hoodies and cargo pants. I grabbed waterproof jackets from a rack near the wall and put them into the cart as well. When I had raided most of the men's and women's clothing section, leaving behind only the children's clothing, I positioned the full cart near the door to the docks.

Taking a second cart, I loaded it with wetsuits, diving masks and snorkels. If we were going to spend a long time at sea, these things would be useful. I read a zombie novel once in which the main character used a wetsuit as protection against bites and scratches. No reason why it wouldn't work. I added swimming trunks and bathing suits to the cart and picked up some pairs of sunglasses.

Pushing the cart to the back of the shop, I found a food shelf and loaded up with pots of dehydrated noodles and three bags of the sugar Elena had requested. I found coils of strong thick marine rope and looped one over my shoulder. I slung a large pair of binoculars around my neck. They looked more powerful than Mike's.

A closed glass cabinet in the fishing section caught my eye and I went over to look at the spearguns displayed inside. The cabinet was locked.

Using the handle of a fishing rod, I smashed the glass and reached inside, taking the six guns and all the spears in there.

The cart was full and I was sure I had salvaged everything useful from the store. I wheeled it over to the cart of clothing and left it there. I thought of checking to see if any of the nearby stores on the street held any treasures. How far did I dare I push my luck? The safety of the marine shop and my two carts of plunder had made me overconfident.

I looked out at the street. Rain lashed down from dark clouds. That was going to affect my vision, making a trip across the road even more dangerous. There was no point looking out for zombies if I was blinking rain out of my eyes every two seconds.

Taking a diving mask from the display, I put it on and pulled up the hood of my jacket. With the mask on, I could keep my eyes open. Pulling up my scarf to cover my lower face, I pushed the door open and stepped out onto the street, gun in hand.

The rain bounced off my hood and the mask but at least I could see. I looked along the street in both directions.

Nothing.

Fifty feet away, I saw the open doorway of a supermarket. It looked like the door had been smashed. The place had probably already been looted but it was worth a look.

I strode across the street quickly.

As I approached the broken door, I lifted the gun and stared into the darkness of the supermarket.

What I saw made me gasp and step back.

Too quickly.

I stumbled and fell, scrambling to regain my feet before the dozens of zombies I had just seen came pouring out of that supermarket like a tidal wave of rotting flesh.

I ran back toward the marine shop, praying I had time to get my carts and wheel them out to the Big Easy before the shambling Nasties caught up with me.

But when I glanced over my shoulder, expecting to see monsters, I saw an empty street.

They hadn't followed me.

I stopped and stood in the road, watching the door of the supermarket.

I heard groans coming from inside but none of the zombies stepped out through the doorway.

Slowly, carefully, I walked back to the doorway and risked a glance inside.

The shop was full of them, packed in there so tightly it was standing room only. They shot hateful looks at me with their yellow eyes and a collective moan rose from the herd. The ones standing closest to the door reached for me but none of them made a move.

I watched them, the prey regarding the predator, and wiped rain from the lenses of the diving mask.

This made no sense.

Either way, the supermarket was a bust.

Out of curiosity, I went to the Chinese restaurant next door and looked in through the windows. The place was full of zombies.

I turned on my heels and went back to the marine shop. Opening the back door and pushing the carts outside, I took a last look around the place to make sure I hadn't missed anything valuable.

Mike stood by the Big Easy waiting for me. When he saw the carts, he came running along the jetty and took one of them from me, pushing it to our boat as I followed.

"You look like a bandit, Man."

"It's easier to see this way."

"See any zombies?"

"Plenty."

He looked over his shoulder and increased his pace.

"Don't worry, they're not coming," I said. I was pretty sure I understood why the city seemed deserted. Why we hadn't seen any zombies during our night in the cave. And why they had seemed to be waiting for us on the porch at the farmhouse.

We reached the Big Easy and managed to unload both carts into the living room area. By the time we were done and the carts on the jetty were empty, the sky had begun to clear a little.

Mike untied us and jumped on board. "Let's go, Man,"

"Just take us out a little," I said. "I want to see if my theory is correct."

"Theory?"

I nodded.

"OK, Man." He climbed up to the bridge and started the engines. We sailed away from the marina, our wake bobbing the moored boats up and down like fishing floats indicating a bite.

When we got half a mile out, I shouted up to Mike, "Stop here."

He cut the engines and the clanking of the chain began as the anchor lowered.

"What is it, Man?" He slid down the ladder and stood beside me.

The rain was stopping. I removed my diving mask and stood watching the marina.

Lucy and Elena came out from the kitchen. "What's going on? Why have we stopped?"

"Alex thinks something's going to happen," Mike informed them.

"What?" Lucy asked.

"Just wait and see," I said.

We stood on the deck while the sea lapped against the side of the boat. The dark clouds that had hung over the city scudded away further inland and the sun broke through. Sunlight hit the boat and we basked in its warmth. The sea shimmered like glass.

"Look," I said, pointing at the marina.

A lone figure moved stiffly out over the jetty. Then another. Within minutes the place where we had been standing earlier was swarming with zombies. The streets erupted with movement as the monsters came staggering out of the shops. Soon the city, which had been deadly silent, was a writhing mass of rotting undead bodies. Their mournful groans reached us even across the half mile of water.

"I don't understand," Lucy said, "How did you know this would happen?"

"It's simple," I said, watching the monsters roam the city. "They won't come out in the rain."

Fifteen

E SAT AROUND THE DINING table with the lights on in the cabin. Darkness had fallen outside. Mike had piloted the Big Easy out a few miles from shore and for the first time in a long while, we felt safe. Elena and Lucy had arranged the food in the cupboards and made chicken curry and rice. Even though the curry came from a can, it filled the dining room with mouth-watering smells of savory spices.

The clothing and supplies from the marine shop had been stowed in the storage rooms below. Mike and Elena had claimed the largest bedroom on the stern, leaving Lucy and me with the smaller helm bedroom. Lucy wasn't complaining about the arrangement. I tried to keep my celebration hidden by fixing a nonchalant look on my face.

The curry was delicious and when we pushed the empty plates away, Lucy said, "Now tell us how you knew about the zombies and the rain."

I had kept quiet on the subject, working it through in my own mind before I was ready to explain it to the others. "I saw a TV show about how a virus behaves. Once it infects a host, it makes the host do things that achieve the virus's goal of spreading to other hosts. There was a virus that made ants climb up high plants so the virus spores would spread further when released. There was a bird virus that started out in a fish but really wanted to be inside a bird. So it made the fish swim erratically in the shallows where it would attract a hungry bird. Once the bird ate the fish, the virus got into the bird where it wanted to be in the first place."

"I don't follow,"Mike said. "How does that apply to zombies and rain?"

"If a virus can make an insect or a fish act like that, it shows that the virus 'thinks' long-term. It makes the host act in ways that will ensure the virus's future."

Mike said, "A virus can't think, Man."

"But it's like thinking. The virus doesn't just infect a host and that's that. If it has bigger plans, it makes the host act according to those plans. So this virus - whatever it is and wherever it came from - wants to spread among humans. Remember that guy who had died of a heart attack in the car crash? There was no reason for the zombies to bite him because he couldn't spread the virus.

It needs the host to be mobile and able to bite or scratch uninfected humans so it can be spread.

"The humans it infects, it kills then raises from the dead. As we've seen... and smelled... the bodies rot. That means they will eventually rot away completely and be useless as hosts. The virus needs to slow that rotting process for as long as it can so the host has a longer 'lifespan' and can infect more victims."

"That makes sense," Lucy said. "Keep the host body as intact as possible. Wet meat attracts microbes. So it makes the zombies avoid the rain."

I nodded. "When those zombies were hiding out on the farmhouse porch, they weren't hiding there waiting for us. They were sheltering from the rain. Cartwright and Brand just happened to go outside while it was still raining and the Nasties were there. That's why they didn't chase us to the Land Rover. The virus wouldn't let them. Rather than take one or two victims at that moment, it wanted to keep the hosts in good condition for longer so they could infect more victims in the future."

"So it makes sense," Elena said, "but how does it help us?"

I had been thinking about that during our meal. "It means that if we have to move overland, we do it when it's raining. We time our raids to coincide with rain and we can move about the streets freely. We'll only have to deal with the zombies inside the buildings we enter. We couldn't even think about entering a city any other way; we'd be outnumbered as soon as we hit the streets. So it gives us a tactic we can use to increase our chance of survival."

"But we aren't going to be raiding cities," she said, "because the U.N. ships are coming, remember? We just need to hold out on this boat until then and we'll be saved."

"We don't know when that will be," Mike said.

"So get on that damn radio and find out. Has anyone even checked the radio lately?" She got up from the table and took her plate over to the sink, throwing it in angrily before going out on deck.

Mike went to follow her. Before stepping out into the night, he turned to us. "This is all getting to her."

"It's getting to all of us," I said to Lucy after Mike was gone, "but she's right. We haven't checked the radio since we heard the emergency broadcast."

"I'll get it." She went below deck to where we had put the rucksacks and came back up with the radio. As I switched it on and placed it on the table, Lucy sat close to me. She had showered earlier and her hair smelled of apple shampoo. Beneath that, I detected a faint hint of her musky perfume.

The radio came on and the EBS played, exactly as before. "Damn," I said, "no change."

"Try the other stations. You never know."

I moved the dial gently, pausing whenever the static seemed to falter, hoping for a transmission. As I was about to give up, a male voice broke through.

"Hey, people, this is Johnny Drake at Survivor Radio wishing you a great evening. Don't let those Nasties get you. Here's a classic tune from Zager and Evans." The song 'In The Year 2525' started to play.

I looked at Lucy. "Survivor Radio?"

She grinned, reflecting the grin I felt on my own face. It was good to hear another voice, to know that somebody was out there somewhere playing music for survivors like us.

Mike and Elena came through the door. "What's that music, Man?"

"Apparently it's Survivor Radio."

They started to dance in the kitchen.

Lucy looked at me and raised an eyebrow. "Shall we?"

I had never danced before but I joined her on the living room floor and gyrated to the music. The next song was 'Break On Through' by The Doors and by now I had gained some confidence and threw out some sixties moves I had seen in movies. Lucy laughed and joined in.

We danced like that for half an hour while Johnny Drake played tune after tune. He sounded like a professional DJ with his smooth voice and slick lead-ins to the music. He even had a station jingle which was, 'Survivor Radio. Lifting the spirits of survivors everywhere.' The music was a mix of everything from old classics to modern rock. Our situation made some of the lyrics even more poignant and we sang along with the songs we knew.

We collapsed exhausted onto the seats and Johnny said, "OK, all you folks out there, it's time for Survivor Reach Out. Want to reach out to a loved one? Need to get a message to a fellow survivor? Contact Survivor Reach Out. You know how."

Another man's voice spoke. The quality of the recording was bad, as if the man were talking through a walkie talkie and had been recorded on an external microphone.

"My name is Frank Jones and I'm trying to contact my son. His name is Lee. Lee Jones. He was at work in Regent Street when the... when everything went wrong. If anyone sees Lee, please tell him I'm alive. His dad is alive."

Johnny Drake's voice came back, sombre this time. "Survivors, keep a look out for Lee Jones in the London area. Let him know his dad is OK. Lee, if you hear this, go to your nearest Survivors Camp and tell them your name. They'll make sure you get back together with your dad."

I was sure everyone on the Big Easy and Johnny Drake were thinking the same thing. If this man's son had been in London when the virus broke out, he was probably dead. Or wandering around Regent Street as a zombie.

A woman's voice came crackling out of the radio. "My name is Linda Williams. My husband is Jim Williams. He was taking our daughters to school on the morning when the virus hit. The girls are Jessica and Olivia. They're six and nine years old. Please, if anyone sees Jim and the girls, ask them to contact the army. They know which Survivors Camp I'm in. That's Jim, Jessica and Olivia Williams. The school was in the Birmingham area. If you're out there, Jim, please get in contact."

Drake said, "If you have a relative or loved one out there, remember to listen in to Survivor Reach Out every hour on the hour. Now here's Billy Joel and Piano Man."

The music drifted from the radio but I wasn't in the mood to listen anymore. Hearing those survivors pleading to the their loved ones... loved ones who were almost certainly dead or worse... left a sour taste in my mouth. Also, Survivor Radio, or at least the Reach Out slot, seemed to be run by the army. The appeals were telling survivors to go to Survivors Camps. The people appealing were in the Camps already. Was this the military's way of keeping spirits up among the survivors? Giving them hope that they could contact loved ones? It sounded like Johnny Drake was either on the military payroll or being forced to play the Reach Out segments on his station.

There was no news about the U.N. rescue mission.

"What shall we do?" Mike asked. "We don't know where the U.N. ships will land or when. Are we just going to drift out here hoping it'll get mentioned on the radio?"

"I don't think the army are telling anyone about the rescue ships," I said. "It's probably on a need-to-know basis."

"Or those two soldiers you overheard on the radio were just talking bullshit," Elena added.

"That's possible too. Either way, if we just drift out to sea, we won't know anything." I had found a map of Britain in the bridge earlier. Now, I laid I out on the table between the dishes. "We need to figure out the most logical place the U.N. will land so we can be in the area when they arrive."

"It could be anywhere, Man."

"Not necessarily. It depends where the ships are coming from and what the conditions near the ports are like. If the ships come from Europe, they'll be landing on the East coast. Unless the ports are too dangerous. Since the main ports on that coast are near majorly-populated areas, they're probably too risky. So the ships would probably come around Scotland and sail along the West coast.

The main ports on the West are also in densely-populated areas. Except in Scotland or the Isle of Man. Now, if the U.N. ships are coming from America, they would most likely dock on the West coast."

"So it looks like the West coast is the most likely, Man."

"Yes. We don't know for sure but I think it's the best bet. Luckily, we're sailing off the West coast at the moment. The question is which port would they use?" I discounted the Isle of Man because that would require the army to transport all the survivors from mainland Britain to the Isle. The port must be on the mainland but in a less-populated area.

"Scotland?" Lucy suggested.

I looked at the map. It seemed logical. That would mean we would have to sail North along the coast to get into the right area. But the Scottish coastline was huge. How would we know where the ships were headed?

"If we get close enough, we should be able to pick up their radio communications," Mike said. "There's some equipment on the bridge that we can use. But we need to get in range."

It was a long shot. The area we were talking about was huge and we didn't even know the time, never mind the place, that the ships would arrive. So we planned to sail up and down the Scottish cost until we picked up radio communications or saw the ships coming across the Atlantic. I didn't hold out much hope for the plan. Unless we found some more information soon, or even evidence that U.N. ships were actually coming, we would probably spend the rest of our days sailing around the British coast, raiding the mainland for food and supplies. The Big Easy was probably going to become our permanent home.

Even that future looked grim if the rest of the world decided to nuke Britain.

In that case, the Big Easy would become our tomb as we all died of radiation poisoning.

Our chance of finding those ships was slim but it was the only chance we had. We had no other choice. I looked at Mike. "Can you plot a course to get us to Scotland?"

"Sure thing, Man."

* * *

The bedroom that Lucy and I were expected to share was small, wood-panelled, and contained twin beds. After a shower, I changed into one of the t-shirts I had plundered from the marine shop, a black shirt with a green logo that said 'Sail To Your Destiny' above a picture of a sailboat. With the addition of a fresh pair of boxers from the same pile of plundered goods, I felt fresh and energized. I had found some paperback thrillers in the living room and planned to spend a couple of hours reading.

I climbed into bed and lay there for a moment before cracking open the book I had chosen. The swaying motion of the Big Easy lulled me into a sleepiness that crept over me like a heavy blanket.

I closed my eyes and slipped into a dream where I was sailing across miles of ocean to reach an island scorched by nuclear destruction and plagued by zombies.

Sixteen

HEN I GOT UP TOP The next morning, Lucy was on the sun deck looking out over the sea. The sun was already up and the sky was clear. A good day for zombies. Lucy wore a 'Sail To Your Destiny' t-shirt the same as mine. It was long enough to reach down to her knees and I wondered if she was wearing anything beneath it. Her hair blew in the gentle breeze as she leaned on the rail, her eyes on the distant shoreline. The air smelled faintly of sea salt with an underlying tang of rotten meat. Even at this distance from the mainland, we could smell the monsters.

"Hey," I said as I approached, 'did you come to bed last night?"

She looked at me and smiled. I felt my heart melt. "I did. You were fast asleep."

I had really gone under fast last night. The stress of the last few days must have become too much for my body and mind. They had simply shut down. Actually, my mind had stayed active; I could still remember a nightmare of walking across a zombie-infested land which had been ravaged by a nuclear winter. I shuddered. Even when I was deep in the middle of gaming weekends involving the most horrific video games, I never had nightmares like that one.

Lucy saw the troubled look on my face. "You OK, Alex?"

"Yeah, I just had a nightmare last night."

"Me too. Then I woke up and realized it was real."

"At least we're still alive."

She stared at the dark shape of the coastline. "Sometimes I think we might be better off dead."

"Don't you mean better off undead?"

"No, not one of them. They seem so tortured. I mean really dead. At peace."

I didn't like the way this conversation was going. Lucy was usually so resilient despite the circumstances. There was a lightness about her that lifted my spirits when I felt low. If she spiralled into depression, it wouldn't be long before I followed.

"It's peaceful on the boat," I said, "and we're safe. Those things can't hurt us out here."

"I know. We're lucky to be alive. It's just that I can't shake the feeling that it won't be long before we're fighting to stay alive again."

I went inside and got the radio. Maybe some music would life the mood. It might also wake Mike and Elena. I was anxious to start our journey to Scotland. The sooner we got there, the more chance we had of intercepting those rescue ships.

Lucy saw the radio in my hand as I came back out on deck and smiled.

"Care for some early morning music?" I put the radio on one of the padded benches.

"As long as it's not Survivor Reach Out."

"Yeah, that was a bit depressing." I clicked the radio on and Bon Jovi filled the air, singing about living on a prayer.

Lucy laughed and headbanged along. I did some lame dancing and air guitar, which made her laugh even harder.

"You're crazy," she shouted over the music.

That made me add in even more ridiculous moves to my heavy metal repertoire and as the solo began, I contorted my face into a grimace as I played my air guitar.

Lucy joined me, playing an air guitar of her own and leaning her back against mine as if we were posing on a stage and playing for a crowd.

The song ended and we both collapsed on the bench, breathing heavily.

Lucy looked at me, her blue eyes sparkling in the morning light.

Zombie apocalypse or not, I was glad I was here with her right now.

Something passed between us and I felt for the first time that she might actually like me. Really like me, in the same way I liked her. It had taken the end of the world to happen but I might have actually met a girl who wasn't a red light professional or somebody on an internet hunt for human contact with anybody at all.

She leaned forward slightly, her eyes locked on mine.

I did the same, feeling her breath against my lips.

My heart hammered in my chest.

"For fuck's sake, you two, turn the fucking music down."

The moment was gone. Mike stood in the doorway, his eyes bleary, his hair sticking up in a bed head.

Jimi Hendrix was on the radio singing 'Are You Experienced?'

Lucy and I parted. I felt the loss immediately. Turning to Mike, I said, "We need to get moving, Mike. The sooner we get into Scottish waters, the better."

He looked at us for a moment, his eyes flickering from me to Lucy and back again as if he were trying to figure out a puzzle. "OK," he said, "let me get dressed first. And turn that fucking radio down, Man." He disappeared inside.

Lucy stood up. "I guess I should get dressed too." She went over to the radio and Jimi faded as she turned the volume down. She went inside quickly.

Fuck. Now she felt embarrassed at what had almost happened between us. I didn't blame her, I guess. She was way out of my league and she knew it. We both knew it. Everybody onboard knew it. Even the zombies onshore probably fucking knew it.

I felt like jumping overboard and drowning myself. I had tried to cheer Lucy up and the music had done the trick but then I had let my idiotic expectations get too high. I was crazy to think Lucy could ever go for a guy like me. There was a reason I spent most of my weekends locked away in a fantasy game world. It was time I faced reality.

And now Lucy was ashamed because we had almost kissed. She must be down there looking at herself in the mirror and saying, "What the fuck are you doing? He's an inexperienced geek. Even in this post-apocalyptic world you can do a lot better for yourself."

I went over to the radio and turned it off.

Striding through the living area to the back of the boat, I climbed the ladder to the bridge. If Mike couldn't get up at a reasonable time because he was too busy in bed with Elena, I would get the boat started myself. After all, how hard could it be to get to Scotland? All we had to do was point North and follow the coastline. I couldn't take any more of this drifting and going nowhere.

I sat in the bridge chair and looked at the instruments on the panel. OK, maybe this looked complex but all I needed to do was raise the anchor and start the engine. The keys sat in a cupboard which also contained maps and charts. They had a neon yellow plastic float attached to the key ring so if they fell into the sea they would float and would be easy to see. I took them out and fit them into the ignition.

And stopped myself before I turned them.

I really didn't know what I was doing.

I took the keys out of the ignition and put them back in the cupboard. I looked out at the calm sea and the clear blue sky. Just sit here and try to calm down. No point crashing the Big Easy into Swansea just because you're a loser.

A crackling sound made me jump. It had come from the instruments. I listened carefully.

Crackle

"…Big Easy…" A man's voice. Coming from the radio set that sat on the wall.

I turned up the volume and moved the tuning knob a fraction until his voice came in clearly.

"…Lighthouse hailing the Big Easy. Do you read? Over."

I picked up the handset and pressed the button. "This is the Big Easy, reading you. Over."

"Ah, so you have got the radio on. I've been hailing you all morning. Saw you on deck dancing with your girl."

Saw us? I leaned toward the window and scanned the coastline. To the North, in the distance, the dark shape of a lighthouse rose from a rocky island. If he could see us from there, he must have some powerful binoculars.

"I wondered if you knew the latest news. Over," he said.

"What news is that? Over."

"If you want the details, I'll do a deal with you. Face to face. Not over the radio. Over."

135

I frowned at the lighthouse. Could he see me? Was he watching me even now? "What deal? Over."

"You get me off this rock and we can all be saved. Over."

"I don't understand. What do you mean?" I almost forgot to add, "Over."

There was a static-filled pause then he said, "The Americans are coming to save us. If you get me off this rock, I'll tell you where and when. Over."

I looked at the radio. I didn't want to make a group decision without the others. "I'll have to get back to you in a few minutes. Over."

More static. Then, "Alright, lad, but don't be too long about it. Otherwise, we'll all be dead. Over."

I wondered if he had lost his mind, surviving alone in that lighthouse while the world around him went to hell. "What do you mean? Over."

"After they pick up survivors and get to a safe distance, they're going to drop The Bomb. Over and out."

Seventeen

AYBE HE'S JUST A CRAZY guy who got into the lighthouse and is using the radio to lure us into a trap, Man," Mike said as we sat around the dining table. We had eaten a breakfast of pancakes which Elena had made from some sort of egg powder, flour and long-life milk. They actually tasted good even though they had a rubbery texture. I wasn't sure if that was because of the ingredients or Elena's lack of cooking skills. The mug of coffee I washed them down with was strong and bitter. I usually took two spoons of sugar in hot drinks but had decided to cut down to half a spoon. Sugar was in plentiful supply on the Big Easy at the moment but that situation probably wouldn't last long. We needed to preserve what we had.

Lucy barely looked at me as we discussed the light house. She had dressed in blue jeans and a tight black sweater, her perfect curves amplifying the fact that she was way out of my league. I tried not to think about it.

The radio call from the lighthouse had caused us a problem. Either the man in there knew where and when the rescue ships were going to land, in which case we needed that information, or he was trying to draw us into a trap.

"It doesn't add up, Man. Why does he need us to get him off his island? Where's his own boat? He must have got out there somehow."

"And if all he wants is to use our boat so he can get rescued," Elena added, "he won't care if we're with him or not. What if he steals the Big Easy?"

"He said he wanted to make a deal. I assume the deal is how we know he isn't going to steal our boat."

"Yeah, right," Mike scoffed, "make a deal with a fucking madman."

"We don't know his story, Mike. He could be telling us the truth. If he's stuck in that lighthouse and Britain is going to be nuked, don't we owe it to him to take him with us to the rescue site? Otherwise, we're leaving him there to die."

"A lot of people are dead, Man. A fucking lot of people."

"So we shouldn't care about one more even if we have a chance to save his life?"

He shrugged. "We need to look after ourselves."

"I agree. And if he has information about the rescue mission, we need it."

"And if this is a trap, we could all get killed, Man. We don't know how many people are in that lighthouse. There could be a dozen killers in there waiting to steal our boat."

"So what do we do?" I asked. "Should we vote on it?"

"Fuck that, Man, I'm going to talk to this guy." He got up and strode out to the aft deck.

We followed. The bridge was only big enough for two people so Elena climbed up while Lucy and I stood on the deck. We could hear the radio from here. Mike was talking into the handset. "Hey, lighthouse guy. You there?"

Static.

"Hey, lighthouse guy. You want us to save your ass, you need to talk to me."

Static.

"He isn't even fucking there, Man."

The radio crackled and hissed.

I looked over at the lighthouse. Was he watching us through his binoculars? I felt like raising my middle finger and flipping him off. Maybe that would get a response out of him.

Lucy came over and stood next to me. "Alex, about earlier…"

"Hey, it's OK. Forget it."

"No, I…"

The man's voice came from the radio, cutting through the static. "My name is Eric."

"Well, Eric, I'm Mike. There are six of us on this boat and we want to know what the fuck your deal is."

More static. Then Eric said, "There are four of you."

"Are you fucking spying on us, Man?"

"I can see you. There isn't much else to look at out here. There are four of you. Not six."

"Is that right?"

"Yes."

"Well you'd better tell us about this deal you want to make, Man."

"I need to get off this rock, Mike. They're going to drop The Bomb. I don't want to be around when that happens. There's a rescue mission taking place. I know where and when the ships are going to land. After that, everyone in this area is going to be dead. That includes me and it includes you. All I want is a ride to the rescue site."

"Where's your own boat?"

"That's a long story."

"We have a long time."

"No, we don't."

Before Mike pressed the button to transmit again, I called him. He poked his head over the top of the ladder. "What is it, Man?"

"He said we don't have a lot of time so the ships must be arriving soon. Like it or not, we need information from this guy."

"Alex, he's been spying on us, Man. The Big Easy is the best thing that happened to us since this shit storm went down and now you want to risk her? He said the

Americans are coming to save us didn't he? So if they're heading up this U.N. mission, America must be virus-free. Fuck this guy and his information. We just sail to America."

"And get blown out of the water by the Coastguard as soon as we get there," I reminded him.

"I'd rather take my chances with the Coastguard than with this guy. He's probably working for some band of pirates and luring ships onto the rocks."

Eric's voice came out of the radio. "Are you still there? Over."

Mike looked at me. "I say we ignore him."

"What do you think?" I asked Lucy,

She sighed. "We need the information about the rescue but I don't think we should risk our boat to get it."

Mike pumped the air with his fist. "Yes. Elena, what's your vote?"

"We should make this guy tell us what he knows. What gives him the right to keep it to himself?"

"He wants to live too," I said. "What gives us the right to take the info and leave him to die? And how were you thinking of taking it anyway?"

"We've got a gun."

I shook my head. Even Mike's plan of ignoring the man was better than this. Was this what we had become now? Thieves? Murderers?

"Elena's right, Man. We can't trust him. I say we go over there and fuck him up until he tells us what we want to know."

"Mike, listen to yourself. This isn't you. You don't use violence to solve problems." All his life, Mike had only ever used violence as a last resort, in self defence, or in defending me. I had never seen this side of him before.

He looked at me with hard eyes. "The world has changed, Man. It's kill or be killed."

Great. So now he was on a 'survival of the fittest' kick. Where did that leave me, the out of shape gamer geek? How long before Mike and Elena decided I didn't fit into their new evolutionary plan and threw me overboard to fight the sharks for survival?

I looked to Lucy for some common sense but she didn't seem to care that we were entering Lord Of The Flies territory just so long as we didn't risk the boat.

"I'll stay with the Big Easy," she said to Mike. "We can't risk losing her."

He grinned. "Awesome. What about you, Alex? You staying onboard or coming ashore?"

"I'll come with you," I said reluctantly. I didn't have much choice if I wanted to stay part of this group of survivors. It felt like the rules were changing by the second and I couldn't let myself be the outcast. So just like when I was at school, I went along with the stronger kids to ensure my own survival.

"Cool." Mike went back into the bridge and keyed the radio. "Yeah, we'll talk with you."

"We can talk when I'm on your boat, OK?" The calmness that had been in Eric's voice earlier seemed to be breaking. Maybe he *was* going mad up there.

"No," Mike replied, "we're coming to see you."

"Listen, you don't understand…"

"See you in a few minutes, Man." Mike turned off the radio and Eric's voice was silenced.

The Big Easy's engine started up and the anchor chain clanked as it drew the anchor up from the sea bed.

I felt a nervous anticipation run through my body as we started moving toward the lighthouse.

Like it or not, we were going in hard.

And nothing would ever be the same again.

Eighteen

IKE BROUGHT THE BIG EASY to a stop a quarter mile out from the lighthouse. As we rocked in the ocean, our own wake hitting the stern, I inspected the lighthouse for signs of danger.

It rose from the rocks like a white cylinder. Windows were placed at various levels and at the top, the huge light sat like an eye looking out over the sea. It reminded of the eye of Sauron from Lord Of The Rings. Around the light ran a balcony and leaning over the railing was a dark-bearded man dressed in green waterproof trousers and a dark blue sweater. He waved at us and shouted. "Let me come aboard."

Mike snorted. "Yeah, right." He turned to us. "OK, here's the plan. Lucy stays with the Big Easy and we take the row boat to the island. I've got the gun. If that fucker tries anything, he'll be sorry. Alex, where's that rope you got from the marine store?"

"In the hold but…"

"Go get it."

There was no point arguing. I went below deck to fetch the rope I had slung over my shoulder at the marine store. I had no idea then that we would be using it to tie up a man. If I had known, would I have still brought it aboard? Depressing as the answer was, I knew I wouldn't have done anything differently.

Mike's earlier reference to the survival of the fittest hadn't just been an off the cuff remark. The world as we knew it had ended. Survival was a prize that had to be fought for. Mike's tactics may seem barbaric but the world had slipped into a new reality. I didn't know where I fit into the new world order but at the moment I was with people who could thrive in it. I had to keep my head down and survive the best I could. At the moment, that meant following Mike's plan to get the information we needed from Eric.

I took the rope up to the aft deck and threw it over the stern railing into the rowboat.

"You need a weapon, Man," Alex said. He had the gun in his hand and Elena had the hand axe.

"I'm fine," I said.

"I'm not taking you ashore unless you have a weapon, Man. What if it's a trap and there's ten guys in there?"

I sighed. I had seen a wooden baseball bat in one of the storage closets earlier. I went to get it. Returning to the deck with my weapon, I said, "Let's go," before tossing the bat into the rowboat.

Mike started down the ladder to the rowboat, Elena close behind. Before I set foot on the top rung, Lucy came over to me.

"Be careful, Alex."

"I will. Look after the Big Easy."

She smiled and I started down the ladder. I felt a cold knot in my stomach. As I sat in the rowboat, Mike took the oars and grinned. "Hey, lighten up. Everything will be OK."

I nodded and gave him a thin-lipped smile.

On the lighthouse balcony, Eric seemed as resigned to what was going to happen as I was. He grimly turned from the railing and went inside.

As we rowed across the water to the rocky island, I was glad I had brought the baseball bat along. Mike was right, there could be a dozen men in there waiting to ambush us and take our boat. It was better to have a fighting chance than no chance at all.

The lighthouse looked much bigger as we approached it, towering above us like a finger pointing at the clear sky. The rocks it stood on were closer to the mainland than they had appeared from the Big Easy. Beyond the rocky island, I could see the cliffs and shoreline. Zombies swarmed over the beach, staggering in the sand. Their pitiful moans reached my ears and I wanted to club every last one of them with the baseball bat just to shut them up.

Mike stopped rowing and let the little boat drift to the rocks. He took the anchor, which the previous owner had made out of a bleach bottle filled with gravel, and threw it overboard. The bottle sank and pulled the rowboat back slightly as it settled on the bottom. Mike looked over the side. "It's deep here. We're going to have to swim ashore."

A dip in the icy sea was not something I had planned on today. The jeans, t-shirt, sweater and boots I wore had only recently dried after the last unplanned swim. Salt stains had ruined the clothes but I still preferred them over the t-shirts from the marine store with their nautical slogans. In this post-apocalyptic world, a t-shirt that said 'Sail To Your Destiny' was just depressing.

I looked over the edge of the boat. The rocks dropped straight down into the murky depths. "Why couldn't we tie the boat to the rocks?" I asked Mike. "Then we don't need to get wet."

"Can't do that, Man. A few good waves will crash the boat against the rocks and destroy her. Then we'd have to swim back to the Big Easy."

I looked out at the yacht. That was a long way to swim. I could barely make out Lucy standing on the sun deck, watching us through Mike's binoculars. I felt like waving but repressed the urge.

Mike took off his t-shirt and placed it on his seat. Bare-chested, he slipped into the sea and swam ashore. When he climbed out onto the rocks in his jeans and boots, he looked like a model on a shoot for a cologne commercial.

Only the gun in his hand looked out of place. "Come on," he said.

I removed my sweater but left my Slipknot t-shirt on. It was already ruined by sea water anyway and our display of power might be ruined if I was standing there feeling self-conscious. As I was about to jump in, Mike called, "Throw me the rope, Man."

I tossed it over to him and he slung it over his shoulder.

Elena slid gracefully into the water and breast-stroked toward shore. It wasn't until she climbed out of the water and onto the rocks that I realized she had stripped to her black bra. With her khaki cargo pants, boots and toned physique, she looked like Lara Croft. The axe in her hand enhanced that illusion.

I grabbed the baseball bat, jumped in and came up gasping for air as the cold sea took the breath from me. Using a combination of doggy paddle and breast stroke, I got to the rocks and clambered out of the water. The t-shirt clung to my back like an icy second skin. I stood up and pulled it away from my goose-bumped flesh.

"Careful on the rocks," Mike said, "they're slippery." He climbed up to the lighthouse, Elena close behind. I steeled myself and followed them, the unwieldy bat making the climb difficult.

When I got to the top, I was out of breath and shivering with cold. The little island had been levelled and reinforced with concrete to facilitate the building of the lighthouse. We stood at the base of the building and looked toward the beach.

"There's a hell of a lot of zombies over there, Man."

I nodded. Although the lighthouse was built on an island, it was no more than a quarter mile from the mainland. And the water separating us and the beach looked shallow. The monsters on the sand could see us and they came to the water's edge, staring at us with their dead yellow eyes.

"They won't go into the sea," I said. "If the virus compels them to protect themselves from rain, they won't go walking into salt water."

"I hope you're right, Man."

"If I wasn't, they'd be wading toward us right now. Look at the hunger in their eyes."

Mike shouted at them, "You fuckers. You want some of this? Come and get it." He laughed and watched them react to the sound of his voice. More of the things came from distant parts of the beach and gathered at the water's edge.

"Look at them," Mike said, "stupid fuckers. I'm not scared of them."

"Mike, we should meet with Eric," I reminded him.

"Yeah. I'm not scared of him either." He strode to the metal door of the lighthouse and banged on it with the butt of the gun. "Hey, open up."

"It's open," Eric shouted from inside. He sounded distant, like he was a few floors up shouting down at us.

Mike looked at us and tried the metal handle on the door, pressing it down. Elena held her axe ready and I had the baseball bat in both hands. I wasn't sure I could actually hit a person with it; I hoped I wouldn't have to find out.

The door clicked open and swung outward. We stepped back, ready for whatever waited inside.

My heart pounded and the cold I had felt a few minutes ago was gone. All my attention was focused on the interior of the lighthouse.

The circular room beyond the door was empty. Coats hung on hooks and boots stood beneath them but there was nothing else there. A circular steel staircase led up to the rooms above.

"Eric," Mike shouted, "where are you? It's Mike."

"Up here," Eric shouted back.

I didn't like this one bit. Why was he up there waiting for us? Why hadn't he come down? If he wanted to leave the lighthouse, he had to come down at some point. There was no other door, only the one we had come through.

"Why don't you come down?" Mike shouted. "Is this any way to treat your guests?"

"You come up."

"Should we close the door?" I asked Mike.

He shrugged. "Why? There's nobody else on this shitty piece of rock. Leave it open in case we need to get out of here fast."

We moved to the base of the steps.

Mike put his boot on the bottom step and I grabbed his shoulder, stopping him. "This doesn't feel right," I whispered.

He held the Colt up in front of my face. "Don't worry, Man." He ascended the steps, gun held in both hands, eyes darting around as if he expected Eric to come jumping out from somewhere up there.

I didn't share Mike's gung-ho attitude. I wished I had stayed on the Big Easy with Lucy but Mike was my friend. As well as having something to prove, I wanted to look out for him. We went back a lot of years and what he had done for me meant a lot. Even so, my stomach was going crazy with butterflies and my mouth felt dry. My heart hammered in my chest and my breathing was fast. The baseball bat felt like lead.

Don't panic.

There's just one guy up there.

Mike has a gun.

We'll be OK.

I followed my friend and Elena took the rear.

We ascended to the first room, a living area with a wood-burning stove, sofa, easy chair and bookshelves. No sign of Eric. Mike stood on the steps waiting for us. He looked eager to find the lighthouse keeper.

"Keep up," he whispered as he went up to the next level.

I looked down at Elena, wondering if she was as eager to find Eric as Mike seemed to be. Coming here in force had been her idea after all.

"Move it, Alex," she urged.

I looked back up. Mike had disappeared around the curve in the steps.

Then I heard a gunshot.

Nineteen

IKE!" I RAN UP THE steps, all thoughts of self-preservation blown out of my head by the fact that my friend was in trouble.

I reached the room above. The kitchen. Eric stood behind the kitchen counter with a shotgun in his hands.

Mike was flattened against the wall by the steps. The shotgun had blown a hole in the wall inches from his head. The air smelled of gunpowder.

"Get back," Eric commanded, "or your friend dies."

I halted on the top step. "You OK, Mike?"

"Yeah, Man."

"Now we're all getting out of here," Eric said. "We're going back to that boat of yours."

"What's the hurry, Man? We can talk about this."

Eric shot a glance out of the window. "There isn't time to talk. Either you take me back to your boat with you or I shoot you and go back by myself."

Elena whispered into my ear, "If we rush him, we can take him down."

I was about to protest, thinking how much ground we had to cover between us and Eric, but she was already counting down.

"3...2...1...Go!"

She gave me a push and I went sprinting forward, bat held in front of me in both hands. Eric jerked his head in our direction and surprise crossed his face. He swung the shotgun so the muzzle pointed at us and he fired. The blast sounded like an explosion in the confined space.

Ears ringing, I jumped up onto the kitchen counter and slid across it on my butt, pushing the bat into Eric's face. He managed to twist away and lifted the shotgun again.

This time I swung the bat at his stomach. It connected and he went down with a groan. The shotgun clattered away across the floor.

I considered delivering another swing but he was down and out, holding his stomach and gasping for breath.

Elena was writhing on the kitchen floor, holding her leg where a gash in her jeans revealed a bloody wound. Mike was holding her, telling her everything was going to be OK. He looked at me with tears in his angry eyes. "I'm going to kill that fucker. He shot Elena."

He came over the kitchen counter in one swift movement and pointed his gun at Eric's head. "You shot my girlfriend, you fucker."

Eric shielded his face with his hands, cowering away from the muzzle of the gun. "Listen to me. We have to get out of here. I'll explain everything when we get to the boat."

"The boat? You aren't getting on our boat."

"The bombs," Eric pleaded, "they're going to drop the bombs."

"You won't be around to see that," Mike said coldly.

I put a hand on Mike's shoulder. "You can't kill him, Mike. We need to know where those ships are going to be."

Mike turned on me. "He shot Elena, Man."

"Yes, and we need to get her back to the Big Easy as soon as possible. Her wound needs to be bandaged up. We're wasting time here. We can tie him up and take him with us, interrogate him later."

Eric looked at me with hope in his eyes. He really wanted off this rock. And fast.

Mike glanced over at Elena. She staggered to her feet, pain etched on her face. Leaning heavily against the wall, she looked at Mike and said, "Kill him. We don't need him. We can find the rescue ships ourselves."

Mike nodded.

He lifted the gun.

Pointed it at Eric's head.

"Wait! There's something you need to know." Eric's eyes were wide. Sweat had broken out across his forehead.

"Talk," Mike said.

Eric pointed a shaky finger at the window. "Look out there."

I went to the window and the sight outside made my blood run cold. The water between us and the mainland was gone, leaving a cement causeway connecting the lighthouse to the beach. All of the zombies from the beach were making their way to the lighthouse. There were dozens of them.

"What is it?" Mike asked.

"We're connected to the beach," I said. "This isn't an island at all. It's tidal. At low tide, there's a causeway." I looked at him and I knew there was fear in my eyes. "The tide's gone out. The zombies are coming."

A sound from the ground floor came drifting up the steps. Shuffling feet. Low moans.

"They're here," Eric groaned.

"How do we get out of here?" Mike asked him, shoving the gun into his temple.

"There's no other way. Only the door downstairs." He looked up at Mike and sneered. "I'm not the only one who's going to die."

"Why the fuck didn't you tell us to close the door? Warn us?"

"You'd have sailed away and left me here. If we'd made a deal we could have gotten off here together. Now we're all going to die. Go ahead and shoot me."

Elena cast a glance down the stairs. "What do we do?"

The only way to go was up. The lighthouse had no doors so we couldn't barricade ourselves inside a room and wait for the zombies to leave.

They were coming up and they would find us.

The moans on the steps became louder.

They could probably smell us up here.

"We need to go up," I said.

"Not him," Mike said, indicating Eric.

"What? You can't leave me here for those things to find me."

"It might buy us a little more time," Mike said. He shot Eric twice, once in each leg. The lighthouse keeper screamed, clutching his wounds.

I didn't judge Mike's actions. We were all dead anyway. It was just a matter of time.

While Eric continued screaming on the kitchen floor, we left him and went up to the next level. Elena leaned on Mike for support and I followed, glancing over my shoulder every now now and then expecting to see a zombie reaching out for me. Luckily they were slow and stairs seemed to slow them down even more.

We reached the bedrooms and continued up to the level above.

I wondered what Lucy would do when we didn't return. She was a survivor, I was sure she'd be alright. The only regret I had was that I would never know what had become of Joe and my parents. This was the time to face facts; they were probably lying dead somewhere, victims of the apocalypse.

And I was about to join them.

One more victim of the zombie outbreak.

Below us, Eric's screams of pain were suddenly replaced with a panicked, "Oh my God! No! No!"

The zombies had reached him.

His cries turned into screams of agony which suddenly cut off.

We ascended the steps to a radio room. A large radio sat on a wooden table. Papers and charts littered a shelf on the wall and a black hardbound log book and pen sat on the table. While Mike and Elena went up to the next level, I grabbed the log book from the table and stuffed it into my jeans. If Eric had learned about the U.N. ships from the radio, he might have written details in the book. It didn't even matter now but something made me take that book.

I followed Mike and Elena up to the top level.

The stairs terminated in a small featureless room. A steel door led out onto the balcony. We went through the door and I closed it. There was a lock but no key. Enough force from the other side would break the latch easily. Of all the places I had thought I might die, on top of a lighthouse had come pretty far down the list. I leaned over the railing and looked down, immediately regretting it as my stomach lurched. It was a long way down. I stepped back.

In the distance, I could see the Big Easy floating calmly on the still sea.

A bang on the door made me flinch. A second bang followed, then a third until the door was being beaten constantly by hungry fists.

I wondered if Lucy could see us through the binoculars. I didn't want her to see me getting ripped apart by zombies. I would rather jump to my death on the rocks below.

Mike was leaning out over the rail and I wondered if he had the same suicidal tendencies. "We can jump," he said.

"It's either that or get ripped to pieces," I replied. "Getting splattered on the rocks might be the quickest way to go."

"No, Man, we can jump into the sea."

"Are you crazy?"

He went to the railing. "If we jump from here, it's straight down into the water. It's plenty deep enough down there. We can do it, Man."

The door buckled beneath the pounding fists.

There was no choice. The zombies would be all over this balcony in a few seconds.

I nodded. "OK."

Elena looked over the edge. "It's totally doable. Mike, you go first and get to the rowboat. Bring it closer for when Alex and I jump.

He nodded, grinned, saluted us and vaulted over the railing. I watched him drop like a rock into the sea below.

After the splash, he surfaced and gave us a thumbs up before swimming to the rowboat.

The door collapsed and two zombies came onto the balcony, many more behind them.

I rushed forward with my bat, swinging it wildly. We needed to slow them down to give us time to jump over the railing. The bat connected with the head of a monster that had once been a businessman judging by his suit and tie. He went down hard and the zombies behind fought to get past the body in their way.

I ran back to the railing. Elena was climbing over, her face a mask of agony as she took her weight on the bad leg.

"You OK?" I asked as I straddled the railing. I tried not to look down. My stomach was flipping crazily and I felt off balance.

"I'm fine," she said, "let's go." She pushed me forward the same way she had done when we rushed Eric. I felt my feet leave the railing and suddenly I was suspended in mid air, the deep sea below me.

Then I fell so fast I barely had time to register it before I hit cold water and heard nothing but a rush in my ears as I went under.

I struggled against the sea, pulling with my arms to bring myself to the surface.

As my face broke though, I breathed in sweet air.

Mike was close by in the rowboat. I swam toward him but his attention was on the lighthouse. He stared up at the balcony and shouted, "Elena!"

I looked up and my heart sank.

For some reason, Elena hadn't managed to clear the railing and now she hung by her hands, dangling over the sea. She looked panicked.

"Just let go!" Mike shouted to her.

She held her breath and let go.

But she didn't fall into the sea.

Hands reached over the railing and grabbed her. Blue-skinned rotting hands.

She screamed as they dragged her back up onto the balcony.

"No!" Mike screamed. He dived off the boat and swum toward the lighthouse. I grabbed him and he struggled against me. "Elena!"

Her screams had been silenced. There was nothing anyone could do.

"It's too late," I told Mike.

His eyes went to the scene on the balcony. The zombies were in a frenzy up there. Tearing. Ripping. Biting.

He looked at me and started to cry. "It's Elena, Man."

"I know." I put a hand on his shoulder. "I'm sorry, Mike."

He looked from me to the lighthouse and for a moment I was sure he was going to swim ashore despite the dozens of zombies on the rocks. Then he went weak and I had to hold him up to stop him from sinking.

Supporting him with one arm and using the other to swim, I got us to the rowboat. He climbed aboard but then sat staring at the sea.

I put the oars into the metal locks and started to row us back to the Big Easy.

My friend stared at the water in a daze and I was sure I would never see the Mike I knew ever again.

Twenty

HE'S BEEN LIKE THAT FOR hours," Lucy said as we sat at the dining table. Her face was still streaked from the tears she had cried for Elena. I was sure there would be more tears but for now she was too drained to shed them.

Outside, evening fell quickly, the darkness spreading over the sea. I had managed to pilot the Big Easy away from the lighthouse. None of us wanted to see that place again. Now we were anchored further North, about two miles from shore. We could still see the city on the coast but at least we couldn't smell it anymore. The sea breeze was fresh and tangy. I felt more removed from those monsters than I had since the apocalypse happened. It was a shame that my feelings of safety were tinged with the darkness of tragedy.

Mike had slumped into the easy chair in the living room when we got back from the lighthouse and had not moved since. I knew his feelings for Elena ran deep but I had never seen him in a catatonic state like this before.

We had already lost one of our group. I didn't know how we would survive if we lost Mike too.

"I don't understand why Eric didn't warn you about the zombies," Lucy said. "It doesn't make sense."

"He was afraid we'd run away and leave him there. He probably stayed zombie-free out there on his rock because when the tide was low it was raining and they weren't around. This was the first time the low tide coincided with dry weather. So suddenly he saw dozens of zombies on the beach and he knew that when the tide went out, they could get to him. That's why he was desperate to leave immediately. If I knew then what I know now I would have brought him aboard the Big Easy straight away. At least Elena would still be alive."

She wiped a tear from her eye. "I still can't believe she's dead."

I looked at the night darkening beyond the windows and my thoughts went somewhere I wished they wouldn't. What if Elena wasn't dead but had been turned into one of *them*? Maybe even now she was roaming the lighthouse in an undead state. I tried not to think about it. There was nothing that could be done.

But there must be something I could do to help Mike. He was hurting in a way I had never seen before. I wasn't going to sit by and watch my friend spiral into depression.

I went to the bar and poured three glasses of brandy. Giving one to Lucy, I went over to Mike and handed him the glass.

He took it with a muttered, "Thanks."

"Hey, why don't we raise a glass to Elena. She was a brave woman. One of the bravest."

Lucy seemed to pick up on what I was trying to do; make Elena's death an event we could remember but also move on from. She raised her brandy. "To Elena. A great friend and a brave survivor."

Mike looked over at her then at me. His eyes were bloodshot. The drink trembled in his hand, spilling over the edge of the glass. "I loved her," he said simply.

"We all did," I said. I took a hit of brandy, feeling it burn all the way down my throat. Mike threw back his glass and downed his drink in one swallow. He resumed his thousand-yard stare, the empty glass forgotten in his hand.

I didn't know what else to do so I went to the bar and got the brandy bottle. I refilled his glass and started back to the dining table. Mike murmured something.

"What's that, buddy?" I asked, turning to face him.

He repeated what he had said but I had the feeling he was speaking to himself. He whispered the words over and over like a mantra.

"They're going to pay."

* * *

Later that evening, after a mostly-uneaten meal of rice and beans spiced with curry powder, I took Eric's log book from where I had put it to dry over one of the portable radiators in the living room. Mike was asleep in the chair as I walked past him to get the book. I hoped he would be feeling better when he woke up.

The only time I saw him express grief in any major way was when his dad died and even then the emotion had only brought forth a few tears. Mike had been a lot younger then. I wondered if his grief over Elena's death was bringing out unexpressed feelings about his father leaving him at a young age.

I sometimes wondered if the reason Mike's life involved the pursuit of activities like rock climbing and hiking was because his father had the same interests. Mike had never never been interested in these things until after his father's death. Maybe he was trying to make his dad proud.

Sitting at the table, I opened the book and flicked through the pages. They were still damp and stuck to my fingers. In places, the pen had smeared but in others it was still legible. The book wasn't meant to be immersed in salt water and was almost ruined after its time in the sea.

The entries I could read contained dates, times, ship names, weather reports and tidal records. Working carefully, I peeled the pages back until I found the last entries Eric would ever write.

Being closer to the middle of the book, these pages were less water-damaged. The handwriting was more readable. It looked like Eric had turned this into more of a diary than a log book.

The last entry read: 'They are back on the beach again. I am only alive because of the high tide. If not for that, they would be over here banging on the door. Still no sign of Harper. I fear he's dead. He would have come back by now. Unless he's left me here. He used to tell me something like this would happen someday but I never listened. I spend most of my time looking out to sea for him or any other boat. I have to leave here soon.'

I skipped back to the previous page. Eric hadn't bothered to date these entries. I got the feeling he was using the log book, something he had developed the habit of writing in every day, as a way to express his thoughts as he became isolated in the lighthouse. I felt sorry for him. At least I had faced the end of the world with three friends. It sounded like Eric had been alone apart from the person he referred to as Harper. And even Harper had left. Why hadn't Eric gone with him?

I scanned down the page.

'Harper has decided to take the boat up along the coast to get a sense of the situation. This is the kind of thing he used to talk about but I don't think even he believes it is really happening. All we receive are garbled radio reports from some of the ships. Even those have stopped now and I fear the ships I see in the distance are crewed by something other then men.'

And further down the page.

'No sign of Harper. It looks like I will be facing this situation alone.'

Then at the bottom of that page I found the entry referring to the U.N. rescue mission.

'Radio picked up a military broadcast. American ships coming to rescue survivors. Everyone moving North to be picked up. I can't be left here alone. I need a boat. I dare not travel by land. The tide is out at the moment but thankfully there is no sign of those things on the beach. I pray for the sea to come back in and protect me again.'

My heart sank. He hadn't written down the location of the rescue. He said North, which probably meant Scotland, but that didn't help. We were heading that way anyway. Without a specific location, we would be drifting around aimlessly off the Scottish coast. I flicked back through the pages but the other entries were all in the standard report format before the apocalypse.

Lucy came over from the kitchen carrying two bottles of beer. "Anything?"

"Nothing. He wrote that the rescue will be in the North but that's all."

She took a swig of beer. "Do you think if we let him onboard he would have taken us to the rescue site?"

"From what I read in here he was just scared and lonely. There was someone called Harper in the lighthouse with him. Harper took their boat up the coast to find out what was happening and never returned. I think Eric was being honest when he said he wanted to make a deal with us. He just spooked at the last minute and tried to use his shotgun to make sure he ended up on the boat. He knew the tide was going out and the zombies were on their way."

"What happened in there, Alex?"

I shrugged. "Mike lost it when Elena got shot. I think we approached the situation the wrong way. We went in with force. If we had dealt with Eric the way he wanted, we'd probably be on the way to being rescued now. And we'd all be alive."

She nodded and took another drink of beer to stop herself from crying. "Do you think Mike is going to snap out of it?"

"I don't know. We'll have to see how he is when he wakes up."

With tears in her eyes, she stared at the night beyond the window. "This is never going to end is it? Things aren't going to get any better. I put the radio on when you left for the lighthouse and the Reach Out came on. All those people looking for loved ones they'll never find. They won't ever know how they died or even if they *are* dead. Their relatives could be out there wandering around as zombies, spreading the disease. And none of it is going to get better. They're just going to bomb the country. It's like they want to wipe the slate clean but they're wiping away all those lives and memories." She started to cry, her face in her hands.

I put an arm around her and she leaned into my chest. She was right. The world would never be the same again. There was no going back from this. Whether the virus was man-made or nature's attack on our species, the human race would never recover.

We went to bed and lay in the darkness fully-clothed, holding each other against the pain and sense of loss.

We both cried for what was gone.

I cried for my parents, for Joe and for Elena. I even shed a tear for Eric. He hadn't been trying to steal the Big Easy, he was just as frightened as we were. He was simply trying to survive.

We fell asleep in each others' arms, two lost souls surrounded by a vast sea of darkness.

It wasn't until the early hours of the morning, as sunlight started to seep in through the windows, that we were both startled awake.

Something big had bumped into the Big Easy.

Twenty-one

WENT UP TO THE aft deck, rubbing sleep from my eyes. Mike was still dead to the world in the easy chair.

The room smelled of curry and beer as I walked through to the deck. Dark clouds were forming further out to sea. The sea was calm at the moment, rolling gently beneath the Big Easy and lifting her into a slow rocking motion. I leaned over the side and looked toward the bow.

A second yacht floated on the water in front of us.

I walked through the dining room to the bow, picking up my baseball bat as I went.

The first thing I thought of was pirates.

These were lawless times. The military exerted some control on the mainland but the sea was a no man's land. We knew there must be pirates out here somewhere. Had they finally found us?

I stepped onto the sun deck, bat clutched in my hands.

Lucy joined me, holding the Colt gingerly. "Is there anyone on board?"

"It doesn't look like it."

The yacht was smaller than the Big Easy. Her name, written across her hull in green script, was The Hornet. She had collided with our bow and floated away about twenty feet. Her engines were dead and everything was silent but a creepy atmosphere hung over her.

"What do you think?" I asked Lucy.

"Looks like she's been floating out here with no crew."

"So how did she get out here?"

"Maybe she came loose from her moorings at the marina and just floated away."

It was possible.

But unlikely.

It was more likely that the Hornet had been piloted out here and something had happened to the crew.

They were either dead or turned into monsters. And they might still be onboard.

"We could just let her float away," I suggested. After our experience at the lighthouse, I didn't see any reason to risk our lives just to explore a ghost ship. The possible rewards were far outweighed by the deadly risk.

Lucy nodded. "I think that's the best idea."

I was glad Mike was still asleep inside. I was sure he would insist on going onboard the Hornet. I had zero desire to explore that eerie ship.

"Back to bed?" Lucy suggested.

I took a glance at the Hornet. She was floating away slowly on the gentle waves. She wasn't going to bump into us again. "Bed sounds good."

We turned to the door and I held it open to let Lucy inside.

Then we heard it.

A bang.

From the Hornet.

We both froze and looked over at the boat.

Another bang came from inside. It sounded like someone slapping their hand against a wooden door.

"We don't have to investigate that," I said.

She bit her lip. God, she was so cute. "What if someone's trapped below deck?"

"The only thing trapped below deck on there is probably a zombie. We should let it go."

I thought she was going to agree with me. I looked forward to getting back to bed. It was still way too early to get up, never mind explore a zombie-infested boat.

Lucy didn't agree. She said, "What if it's a person on there? What if they need our help?"

I sighed. The bed suddenly seemed an unfathomable distance away. "What are you suggesting?"

"We could check it out. We don't have to go onboard. We could row up to the Hornet and look through the portholes. If it's a zombie, we let it drift away."

It sounded safe enough. I hoped that whatever was onboard the Hornet could be seen from the portholes. At least we'd know what we were dealing with.

"Only one of us should go," I said. "In case Mike wakes up. I don't want him to wake up and be alone."

"I'll go," she said.

I didn't see any reason to argue with that. It wasn't like I had to step up to the plate and volunteer for Lucy's protection. Looking through the portholes of a boat wasn't exactly dangerous. Besides, she was capable of looking after herself. I just hoped she saw a zombie through the window. Then we could forget about the Hornet and let her drift away.

We went through to the aft deck, passing a sleeping Mike. Lucy climbed down into the rowboat and I handed her the baseball bat. "Take this."

She held up the Colt. "I've got the gun. I don't need the bat."

"I'll get a speargun and cover you." I was dying to try them out but hadn't had the chance yet.

"Don't point those things anywhere near me. I'll be fine."

"Just promise me you won't go onboard."

"I promise. This is just a reconnaissance mission."

I untied the rowboat from the Big Easy and went back through the boat to the sun deck to watch her. She waved as she came into view then put her back into the rowing. The Hornet had drifted thirty feet away now. Lucy rowed half the distance then shouted to me, "Throw me the mooring rope."

I frowned at her. "Why?"

"If I tie her on, she won't drift away. Otherwise I might have to row half a mile to get back to the Big Easy."

She had a point. I picked up the thick rope, swung it a couple of times to get momentum then let it go. It snaked across the water and landed a few feet from the rowboat. Lucy fished it out of the sea with an oar and coiled it by her feet. She rowed the rest of the distance to the Hornet and tied the rope around one of the aft railings.

Even being connected by a rope felt like too much contact between us and the Hornet.

The banging had stopped and the Hornet was quiet again. But the silence was unsettling.

Lucy knelt in the rowboat and used her hands on the hull of the Hornet to pull herself to the first porthole. She peered inside. After a few seconds she pulled herself along to the next porthole and shielded her eyes from the sun as she looked through the glass. The Hornet had four portholes on this side and after Lucy had inspected the interior of the boat through each one, she rowed around the other side to check there. I waited until she reappeared around the stern.

"Nothing," she shouted. "Should I climb aboard and have a look?"

Sudden panic rose in me like acid in my throat. "No! Come back and we'll decide what to do next."

She stood in the rowboat and grabbed the edge of the Hornet, craning her neck to see over onto the aft deck. "It looks deserted," she said.

"Lucy, come back!" If she went onboard, I was going to have to jump in and swim over there. I couldn't let her go onto the Hornet by herself. It might look empty from the windows but that meant nothing.

She reached up as if she was going to pull herself up onto the deck.

"Lucy, you promised!"

She stopped and looked over at me.

Hesitated.

Sat back down in the rowboat and made her way back to the Big Easy.

I breathed a sigh of relief but I knew this wasn't going to be as simple as untying the Hornet and letting her float away. Lucy's curiosity had gotten the better of her and she wanted to investigate. I felt like cutting the rope now and watching the Hornet disappear into the distance. That would be that. But that would just delay the inevitable. At some point we were going to have to raid the mainland for food and then we would have to deal with zombies. Maybe facing one or two on a boat was a good way to get us ready for that confrontation when it came. The world was full of monsters now and there was no way we could avoid them forever.

Lucy shouted me from the aft deck. I went back there, the baseball bat feeling heavy in my hands. It looked like I was about to face a nerve-shredding situation again. I would have thought that after playing hundreds of video games involving sneaking around and trying to avoid enemies, I would be prepared for this kind of thing. But my games had only prepared my nervous system so far. Just the thought of going below deck on the Hornet made my palms feel sweaty and my hands tremble.

I climbed into the rowboat and took the oars from Lucy.

As I rowed toward the Hornet, I couldn't shake the feeling that something really bad was about to happen.

Twenty-Two

I STOOD ON THE DECK of the Hornet, bat ready in my hands, while Lucy climbed up to join me. The boat swayed gently beneath my feet but there was no other movement. No zombie rushing at me from inside, yellow eyes blazing. Even the banging we had heard earlier had stopped and the eerie quiet had descended over the yacht again.

"Anything?" Lucy asked as she stood next to me.

"I wouldn't be standing here calmly if I'd seen anything."

"That's true." She stepped to the door that led below deck and turned the handle. The door opened slowly with a slight creak. A small flight of wooden steps led down to living quarters.

I sniffed the air. It smelled stale and underlying the staleness was a hint of decomposition. Lucy wrinkled her nose. "Something's dead down there."

I could deal with the dead. It was the undead I wanted to avoid.

Lucy went down the steps with the gun held up in front her face. I followed, leaving the door open behind me to let fresh air into the cabins and cleanse the stench of death.

Lucy poked her head around a doorway and said, "He's in here." She stepped into the room and I took a quick glance along the corridor before joining her.

It stank worse in here and that was because of the corpse on the bed. He was a man in his thirties. He had a neat hair cut, linen shirt, jeans and what looked like a real gold Rolex on his left wrist. In his day, this man had been wealthy. But his day was gone and there would be no more. On the nightstand, an empty bottle of pills and a drained bottle of whisky told the story. In case we didn't get it from the booze and tranquilizers, he had left a note on the bed next to his body. I picked it up and read it out loud.

"Mary and Dan have changed. I have locked them in the store room. I can't live without them. Max Prentice."

I looked over the paper at Lucy. "He said he locked them in the store room. They're still on board." Instinctively, I glanced at the door, expecting this dead man's wife and son to come staggering in, reaching for us.

"Why can't we hear them banging anymore?" Lucy asked.

I shrugged. "If they know we're here, why aren't they going crazy to get to us? I'd at least expect banging on the door if they're locked in somewhere. Why are they being quiet?"

"You're the zombie expert, you tell me."

"I don't know." Were they lying in wait for us? I had assumed that the zombies at the farmhouse hadn't been waiting for us to leave the house... that they had only been on the porch because they were sheltering from the rain... but now I wondered if they had been hiding after all.

A sudden bang from within the boat made us both jump.

I put my finger to my lips and we stood there in the silence that had again descended over the Hornet. I wanted to get out of this room of death more than anything but I needed to know if my theory was correct. I tried to put myself in the shoes of the virus. It wanted to spread. If it was trapped and unable to infect others, what would it make the host do to increase the chances of escape?

Another bang sounded from along the corridor.

"They're trying to attract our attention," I whispered to Lucy.

"By banging on the door?"

"They're locked in a room. There's no way for the virus to spread. So it's trying to attract the attention of somebody... anybody... to come open the door. They've probably been banging like that since they got locked in there. Just biding their time and waiting."

"Do you think they know we're here?"

"Yeah. They probably want to try and tear that door down to get to us but they know we'd run. So they're luring us to them. Think about it… the only reason we came on board was because we heard that bang. They're using human curiosity to get us to open the door. And if we did that…"

"Curiosity killed the cat," she said.

"Exactly."

"I say we don't open the door."

"Sounds good to me. We should take a quick look around to see if there's anything worth taking before we leave."

We left the last resting place of Max Prentice and went to the kitchen, ignoring a bang from down the corridor.

An empty plastic cool box on the table seemed an ideal way to transport goods back to the rowboat so we set about placing cans inside. There weren't many. I had the impression Max and his family had taken the Hornet out on a weekend cruise. Their pleasure had turned to horror when somebody on board turned. Maybe it was Mary, the mother, saying that morning that she felt well enough to go out on the boat despite being a little sick. Maybe it was Dan, the son, keeping his illness hidden from his parents because he had been looking forward all week to a weekend out at sea.

Either way, the consequences were tragic. A mother and her son turned into monsters. A father, unable to deal with the loss, taking his own life.

"There's not much here," Lucy said, searching the cupboards.

"No, let's go."

"Wait, what's this?" She brought out a gun from the cupboard underneath the sink.

"Flare gun. There's one on the Big Easy too. It's in a cupboard up on the bridge."

She found a box of flares and stuffed it into her pocket along with the gun. "Might as well take them."

"Sure. Although I'm not sure who we'll be signalling."

"You take that box outside and I'll check the other bedrooms."

"Don't go near that storeroom."

She turned to me. "How will I know which door leads to the storeroom?"

"It's the door that's locked."

"Oh, yeah." She went down the corridor to search for more plunder. A loud banging came from down there.

"It's the door that's being pounded on," I shouted after her.

"Got it. Avoid the noisy door."

I picked up the cool box, carried it outside and laid it on the deck. I was about to go back inside to help Lucy search the bedrooms when I heard something break and then a high-pitched scream. I ran in, bat ready in my hands. "Lucy!"

There was banging coming from down the corridor. And that god-awful low moaning.

"I'm in a bedroom," she said, "They're trying to get in. I can't hold the door closed."

I didn't even think. I sprinted down the corridor and around a corner to come face to face with Max's wife and son. They had broken through the storeroom door. It lay in splinters on the floor. They pounded on the door opposite. With every blow from their fists, the door opened slightly and Lucy grunted as she pushed it closed again.

"Hey!" I shouted at the zombies.

They turned their greedy yellow eyes on me.

Mary was dressed in a light brown sweater and jeans just like any normal woman on a weekend getaway with her husband and son. Except she wasn't a normal woman. Her long blonde covered most of her face but the blue skin and yellow eyes were apparent. She opened her mouth and moaned hungrily at the sight of me.

Dan, dressed in a Slayer t-shirt and black jeans echoed his mother's pitiful cry and came for me, staggering forward in the cramped confines of the corridor.

I backed away, hoping to lead them into the kitchen where I could get the space I needed for a good swing of the bat.

They followed. My mouth was suddenly dry and my heart felt like it was beating in my temples. I felt repulsed by these creatures with their stink of death and rabid eyes. They were no longer the wife and son Max Prentice had come onboard with; they were foul monsters, killing machines with a single purpose: destroy humanity.

I backed into the kitchen. They were getting closer, picking up speed as they anticipated the taste of their prey.

I refused to be that prey.

I swung the bat at Dan's head. The wood cracked into his skull, sending him down to the floor.

Mary stepped over her son, her maternal instincts long gone, and gnashed her teeth at me.

I pushed her away with the tip of the bat, giving her a hard shove into the kitchen cupboards. The cupboard doors flung open and plates and dishes fell onto the floor, shattering into a thousand pieces.

Dan got up and lurched forward, his rotting hand brushing my arm. The revulsion rose in my throat like hot bile and I reflexively hit him with the bat again.

I heard his skull crack. The bat sunk into his head and he dropped heavily at my feet.

Mary came at me, pushing me out of the doorway onto the deck. She was a thin woman but she had strength lent to her by the virus that inhabited her body. I fell backwards and she was on top of me, teeth biting and tearing at the air in front of my face.

Her breath smelled like rotted leaves, rancid meat and open graves. I wretched as I fought to hold her head away from me.

Her yellow eyes seemed to bore into my skull with their hatred.

She came in closer, her fetid smell making me want to vomit.

Just as I thought she was going to get close enough to bite me, her body lit up with sparks and flame. Her grip on me loosened and I pushed her away, rolling out from under her and scrambling to my feet.

She staggered backward, her entire body lit up like a firework, flame licking the blue skin. She seemed unable to comprehend what to do and chose to make a final lunge at me.

I hit her with the bat and she went toppling over the back of the boat.

Lucy stepped forward, flare gun in hand.

"Thanks," I said.

"Thank *you* for distracting them so I could get out of the bedroom."

Beyond the stern, smoke drifted into the air. The crackle of flames reached our ears.

"Oh, shit!" I said, leaning over the edge and looking down.

Mary's flaming corpse had landed in our rowboat. As the zombie lay like a heap of flaming rags, the rowboat burned around her.

I untied the rowboat and let her drift away before she set the Hornet on fire.

Lucy looked at the burning boat and sighed. "Looks like we'll be swimming back."

Great. Just what I needed after fighting zombies, a swim in the cold sea. Although it might get rid of the grave smell I felt was clinging to me. I wanted to get back to the Big Easy, burn these clothes and take a shower in disinfectant.

On the water, the rowboat still burned. The zombie corpse emitted a foul-smelling black smoke.

I turned to Lucy. "So was it worth coming aboard?"

She nodded. "Of course. We learned a valuable lesson."

"And what lesson might that be?"

"We learned that flares kill zombies."

"Yeah, it nearly killed me too. You could have just used the Colt."

"Not nearly as dramatic."

"At least we'd still have our rowboat."

"Hey, it was you who hit her overboard, Slugger."

"She was about to kill me."

Her face went suddenly serious. "What are we going to do with Dan and Max?"

"I assumed we would untie the Hornet and let her float free." Their bodies would float around on the boat until it sank or someone else found it.

A voice came from the bridge radio. A man's voice. "Hornet."

We looked at each other and went to the radio. I hesitated before answering. Maybe these were the pirates I had been thinking about earlier.

"Hornet," the voice repeated.

"Should we answer it?" Lucy whispered.

"I don't know. The last time we answered the radio, it didn't turn out well."

The man's voice sounded frustrated. "Come on, you two. Don't just stand there staring at the radio. Pick up."

"What the hell? Can he see us?" I scanned the ocean for boats. Apart from the Big Easy and the slowly-sinking rowboat, the sea was empty. Could it be someone with high-power binoculars? We were too far from the coast to be seen that clearly.

I picked up the handset. "This is Hornet. Who are you?"

"Name's Harper. Frank Harper. I'm the guy with a gun to your friend's head."

"What?"

"Don't take my word for it. Here… listen."

Mike's voice came over the radio. "Hey, Man, I think you'd better get back here."

Harper was on board the Big Easy. While we had been investigating the Hornet, he had boarded our boat.

I looked over to the Big Easy. Mike was sitting on the aft deck, his arms secured behind him. Leaning out from the bridge, radio handset in his hand, a fair-haired man in a black knitted cap, sweater and trousers stared right at me. In his other hand he held a revolver pointed at Mike's head.

"You two get back here. Don't even think about running. Your friend will end up dead."

I felt angry that he had the nerve to try and take over the Big Easy. "What do you want, Harper?"

"It's simple," he said, "we're going to take a trip to a lighthouse."

Twenty-Three

A S SOON AS LUCY AND I climbed out of the cold water and onto the deck of the Big Easy, Harper pointed the gun in Lucy's direction. "You drop that gun and the flare gun you used to finish off that zombie and kick them across this way."

She did as he asked. She had no choice.

"Same with the baseball bat,"he told me.

I tossed it across the deck. It clattered at his feet.

I felt mad at myself at myself for letting this happen. Harper had piloted his boat up to the Big Easy while Lucy and I were on the Hornet, left it on the opposite side of the hull so we couldn't see it, and climbed aboard while Mike was still sleeping. We never should have left Mike onboard alone. I looked at Harper's boat bobbing in the sea. It was filled with boxes, petrol cans and gas canisters. It also had an outboard motor. A means of escape?

I looked at Mike. His hands were tied behind his back with rope. "Are you OK?"

"Yeah, I'm fine, Man." His eyes were dead, his voice flat. He had been forced awake by Harper but he was still in a shock over Elena's death. Whatever happened, I couldn't let Harper take us back to that lighthouse. I had the terrible feeling that Elena was still there, wandering the place in zombie form. If Mike saw that...

"There's no point going to the lighthouse," I said. "It's overrun with zombies. Your friend Eric is dead."

"I know that." He said unemotionally. "I saw it. It was only a matter of time before those things got to the place. Poor Eric should have stuck with me. I told him to come with me and we'd find out what was going on but he wanted to stay at his post, find out what he could from the radio." He pointed at me with the muzzle of the revolver. "Do you know how to drive this boat?"

I nodded.

"So let's weigh anchor and get going."

"I just told you, the lighthouse is crawling with zombies."

"And I told *you* I know that. That's why I couldn't go back on my own. I couldn't take on all those creatures.. But you three... well I just saw you make a flame-grilled zombie burger over there so clearing the lighthouse shouldn't be a problem for you."

There was no way I was going to 'clear' the lighthouse if Elena was in there. And there was no way Mike should even be going back to that area. "What's the point in going back to the lighthouse?" I asked Harper.

"Never mind that. Come on, we haven't got a lot of time. The tide's high at the moment so any zombies on the island are stuck there and no more can come from the beach. In a couple of hours that situation will change when the tide goes out again. So move it. Get us to the lighthouse." He jabbed his thumb at the ladder that led to the bridge.

"What about the Hornet? She's still tied on." I needed to stall him, needed time to think.

"You go untie her," he said to Lucy, "Then come straight back here."

She went through to the front of the boat and I climbed up to the bridge. I watched Lucy through the window as she untied the Hornet and set her adrift. The tragedy of Max Prentice and his family would soon be in our past but I feared a much deeper tragedy in our near future. Lucy stood on the foredeck watching the boat slip away. I wondered if she had any plans on how we were going to get out of this mess. I hoped she did because I was out of ideas.

"Let's go," Harper called from below.

I started the engine and hit the button that retracted the anchor. Turning the Big Easy South, I gave her a little throttle and we glided along. Although we sailed at a sedate pace, my mind raced. I scanned the bridge for weapons then remembered the flare gun in the cupboard. I opened the cupboard and looked inside. There was a First Aid kit and the flare gun along with a dozen flares. I took it out and stuffed it into my wet jeans. Could I really kill a man? Killing zombies was one thing. They were already dead. But Harper was alive. It would be murder.

He seemed willing enough to murder us so why not turn the tables on him?

"Give it more throttle," he shouted up at me.

I increased our speed very slightly and wondered how I was going to make my move. I had to be careful because I couldn't risk setting the Big Easy on fire. I also had to make sure he didn't kill one of us before I could kill him.

I leaned out of the bridge. I had a pretty clear shot at him from here but he was close to Mike, keeping the gun pointed at him.

He looked up and saw me. "What are you looking at?"

"Can I change into some dry clothes?"

"No."

I sat back on the chair. I was cold. I was worried about what we'd find at the lighthouse. Maybe, just maybe, Elena had moved on with her zombie friends and was in Swansea or further inland. I didn't know what motivated the zombies to move around. Sure, they were in search of prey but what made them decide where to go? Did they wander aimlessly?

I thought of Mary and Dan locked in the storeroom on the Hornet. They had waited it out, banging every now and then to see if they could lure a curious person to open the door. When that didn't work, they came crashing through to get us. So they could have escaped at any time but chose to wait. Why? Were they aware that if they came out too soon, we would have left the boat and been beyond their reach? Had they waited until they were certain we weren't going to open the door and Lucy was close enough for them to make an attempt to get her?

So many questions. I had no idea how this virus controlled its hosts. I had picked up on the rain phenomenon and I assumed that applied to all extremes of weather. Maybe the virus would make the rotting host shelter from the sun on a hot day as well. But as far as killing their prey and spreading the virus went, I thought I might have underestimated the zombies so far. They seemed to have reasoning abilities that responded to situations and the environment.

Maybe someday scientists would study them but for now this was a game of survival. Us versus them. Unfortunately our fight wasn't just with the zombies; we were also fighting each other. The military were trying to control the populace and men like Harper were using force to get others to risk their lives. Life had never been fair but this event had tipped it over into a living hell. The people rounded up by the military and put in Survivors Camps were innocent yet they had to endure being treated as if they were prisoners of war captured by an enemy force.

In the distance, I could see the lighthouse. If I was going to stop Harper, I had to do it now.

I looked down onto the deck. He was still too close to Mike. I couldn't risk a shot.

Damn it. I slapped the wall in frustration.

Using the binoculars, I focussed in on the lighthouse and its rocky island. A few shapes moved around the base of the tower but it was getting cloudy and misty along the coast and it made it hard to see clearly.

At least I couldn't see Elena.

Somewhere out at sea, distant thunder rumbled.

A few spatters of rain hit the windshield.

Then more.

Then the heavens opened and the rain came down in a torrent.

I checked the rocks near the lighthouse again. The shapes were gone, obviously taking cover in the lighthouse.

All of the zombies on the island would be in there now, roaming the lighthouse from the ground floor up.

And we were about to go in there with them.

Twenty-four

I DROPPED THE ANCHOR WHEN we were about a quarter mile from the rocks and climbed down to the deck below, blinking against the rain as it lashed my face.

Harper had ordered Mike and Lucy inside and they sat together on the sofa while he sat opposite them in the easy chair, gun pointed at them.

I got in out of the rain and wiped my face. "We're here," I told Harper. "Are you going to tell us what we're doing here?"

"I need something from the safe in my room," he said. "You're going to help me get in there and back out in one piece. When I have what I want, we're done. I'll go my way and you go yours. None of you has to get hurt. But if you try to stop me, I will kill at least one of you, maybe all of you. All you have to do to survive is fight off the zombies in the lighthouse."

"You know it's raining out there?" I said. "Do you know what that means?"

"Yeah, it means they'll all be inside. Zombies don't like the rain."

"You think we'll go in there and come out alive?"

He shrugged. "Maybe not all of us. I'm surprised you've survived this long. You look like the type of person who read zombie novels and played video games before all this went down. That normally doesn't translate well to a real situation."

"What do you know about it?" I said, my anger hiding my acknowledgment that he was right.

"I know plenty. While you were having fantasies about the walking dead, I was preparing. I spent my weekends at gun clubs, at survivalist lectures, at survival exercises in the woods. I knew something like this would happen someday. So I prepared for it. This isn't a fantasy, this is reality."

"If you're so well-prepared, why do you have to go back to the lighthouse? Leave something behind? Doesn't sound so well-prepared to me."

He looked chagrined. "I admit I made one mistake. I should have taken all of my things with me when I left the lighthouse. But I didn't realize then what was actually going down. I thought I'd have time to check out the lay of the land and get back to collect what I needed. It didn't turn out that way."

"What is it you need?" Lucy asked. "What are we risking our lives for?"

"Just a set of keys."

"Keys to what?" I asked.

"My place. The place I've been preparing all this time. It's remote, protected by walls, has enough food and supplies for years. Solar power, hot water, everything. While you're fighting to survive in this hellhole, I'll be living in luxury." He grinned at Lucy. "You could come with me, Love. There's plenty of room for two."

"Go to hell," she said, crossing her arms.

"It's you three that will be going to hell. They're going to nuke Britain. Did you know that? Do you know how to survive in a nuclear winter? You're already dead, you just don't know it yet."

"The U.N. are coming," Lucy said. "They're taking survivors to America."

He snorted. "Is that right? How long do you think it's going to take for the virus to get there? Even if they took you to their shores, it will just be a matter of time before you're living in Zombie America."

"You have to have hope," Lucy said.

"I have hope, young lady, because I don't trust in anyone except myself. You can trust in these rescuers if you want but you'll end up dead. Anyway, we're wasting time here. The tide will be going out soon and the lighthouse will be open to the mainland again. Come on, we're going on a little mission."

"I need to change first," I said, "and so does Lucy." We were still dripping wet from our swim and I felt a chill that reached all the way to my bones.

"Alright but be quick about it."

I headed for the door to the bedrooms and Lucy got up to join me.

"No, no, no," Harper said, waving the gun. "One at a time."

I went down to the room where we kept our clothes and changed into my rain gear... a 'Sail To Your Destiny' t-shirt, dark blue fleece jacket and waterproof trousers I had taken from the marine store. Over that I put on the waterproof jacket Mike had lent me for the hiking trip and a woollen scarf. I grabbed the diving mask to give me better visibility in the rain and went back upstairs.

"Fucking hell," Harper said when he saw me, "you look like you're ready for nuclear winter already."

Lucy went and changed into jeans, a sweater and her jacket and Harper told her to untie Mike. Then he led all three of us out to the aft deck.

"Bring my boat around to the ladder and get in one by one. All of you move to the stern where I can keep an eye on you."

Mike took the rope and guided Harper's boat to the ladder. It was a fair-sized fishing boat but Harper had loaded it with fuel cans and gas bottles so there was hardly any room on the deck. It looked like his preparation was still ongoing. He had boxes stored in the cabin and lashed to the front deck. We climbed aboard and sat among the cartons, boxes and canisters.

Harper dropped onto the deck, told Mike to untie us from the Big Easy, and went into the cabin to start the engine. He pulled away from our boat and steered toward the lighthouse.

Lucy looked at me and I knew she was thinking the same thing as me: how would seeing Elena affect Mike? I gave her an almost imperceptible shrug. When I got changed, I put the flare gun and flares into the inside pocket of my jacket. I couldn't risk a shot now with all the petrol on board Harper's boat; it would go up like a bomb.

The rain washed down on us as we approached the rocks. The sky was gravestone grey. I put on the diving mask so my eyes were more comfortable in the rain.

Harper pulled the boat up to the rocks and told us to get off. We climbed out and stood in the rain while he tossed the mooring rope to Mike. Gathering up an armful of weapons, Harper kept the gun trained in us as he got out of the boat. He tossed the weapons at our feet.

A hand axe, a baseball bat and metal bar.

"Arm yourselves," he said.

Lucy chose the axe and Mike picked up the metal bar, leaving me with the baseball bat. I hefted it and gave it a couple of swings in the air. We were about to go into a lighthouse full of zombies, I wanted to be sure I knew my weapon.

"Right," Harper said, "we're going up to the bedroom level. That's above the kitchen and living room."

"We know," Lucy said, "we've been here before."

I looked over at Mike. He was staring at the lighthouse, the rain falling unnoticed on his face.

"You OK, Mike?" I asked him.

"I don't want to go up there, Man."

I looked at Harper. "Maybe Mike should wait here. His girlfriend…"

Harper laughed. "Wait here? He's the biggest guy among you. You think I'm going to rely on a geek and a girl to keep me safe? This guy is the only reason you're useful to me. There's no way he's staying here while we go inside."

He gestured with the gun toward the lighthouse. "Let's go." While we walked ahead, he stayed far enough behind us to be out of our reach if we decided to rush him.

The door to the lighthouse was open. In the darkness beyond, I could see five sets of yellow zombie eyes watching us. They began to groan as we got closer.

From what I guessed about zombies, I had no doubt that they would come out into the rain if they thought they had a chance of catching prey. The herd I had seen in the supermarket had stayed inside because I was too far away from them to be caught easily. I would run and get away. So their conditioning told them to stay out of the rain.

But the way Mary and Dan had laid their trap on the Hornet, hoping to lure people to open the door, then smashing down the door when that didn't work, made me think that these 'rules' the zombies followed weren't rigid. They were adaptable to specific situations.

In general, they didn't come out in the rain but if there was easy prey they would. It would be in the virus's best interests to infect another human even if it meant quicker decay of the host that it used as an attacker. That host might decay faster after getting wet but now there was a new zombie to help spread the virus. The math made it worth the risk, probably.

So these monsters taking shelter on the ground floor of the lighthouse would wait until we got too close to run away easily and then they would attack.

"Be careful," I said to Mike and Lucy.

Mike was the first to reach the doorway. He swung his steel bar and it slammed into the skull of a zombie in a wetsuit, sending the creature down to the ground like a dead weight.

Two more came staggering out, their primitive senses obviously sensing that we were now close enough to kill. Lucy swung the axe up and it cut through the jaw of a woman in a sun dress. Her face split in two as the axe blade travelled up into her brain.

I stepped forward to deal with the third attacker, a man in a 'Sail To Your Destiny' t-shirt and jeans. I wondered if he was an employee at the marina store. He had no stock to sell now, I had taken it all. I swung the bat as hard as I could at his head. He fell heavily and lay twitching on the ground. His eyes stared at up at me with hared. He was still alive… whatever alive meant to these creatures… but his neck was broken and he couldn't move. He lay there gnashing his teeth at nothing in particular.

The remaining two came staggering out, arms reaching for us. Mike smacked one down with the bar and Lucy axed the other in the top of the head.

We stood in the rain, letting it wash their black blood and blue flesh from our clothing. The smell of death and putrefaction hung thickly in the air.

We went inside and I removed my diving mask before it got misted up. From the floors above, we could hear them moving about, shuffling around and moaning. It sounded like there were dozens of them up there. And I somehow knew one of them was Elena.

I couldn't see my best friend experience the pain of seeing her again. I would do anything to spare Mike that torture.

He was staring up the steps, swallowing hard, He knew she was up there.

Outside, the storm passed over and the rain slowed to a gentle trickle before stopping completely.

"Come on," Harper said from outside the doorway, "Get up the steps. My safe is on the third floor. There's plenty more killing to be done yet."

Mike took a deep breath and put a boot on the lowest step. The pain etched on his face killed me. No more.

I reached into my jacket and gripped the handle of the flare gun. I yanked it out, arced it toward Harper and pulled the trigger.

Twenty-five

THE FLARE SHOT AT HARPER like a rocket, leaving a snaking trail of smoke behind it.

He jumped to one side as soon as he saw me aim the gun at him but the flare was propelled with such speed it hit him in the thigh, sending him tumbling to the cement. He cried out in surprise, clutching his leg. The flare bounced off his trousers and shot up into the sky.

Mike was out the door and on Harper like a wild animal, straddling the survivalist with both legs, fist raised. He hit Harper in the face. The blow made Harper's nose erupt with vivid red blood.

"You fucker!" Mike shouted over and over, bringing his fists down again and again.

"Please." Harper begged, trying to shield his bloody face with his hands, "no more."

"Mike, we need to get out of here," Lucy said. We could hear the zombies coming down the steps from above. We had to get out of here now.

He looked up at us. "Yeah," he said, nodding. "What about him?"

Harper looked pathetic cowering beneath Mike, his face a bloody mess. I had tried to kill him a moment ago but only to spare Mike the pain of seeing Elena. If we didn't move right now and get back to the Big Easy, all that would have been in vain. The zombies were right behind us. Their heavy footfalls thudded on the steps. I tried not to make out Elena's voice among the hungry groans.

"Bring him with us," I said, desperate to leave, "we can deal with him later."

Lucy cast a worried look over her shoulder into the lighthouse. "Alex, we need to go *now!*"

I wondered if she saw Elena back there. I didn't have time to look.

I rushed forward and helped Mike get Harper to his feet. Taking an arm each, we hustled him along to his boat. Lucy took up the rear, urging us to, "Move, move move!" I could hear the zombies behind us, coming out of the lighthouse and shuffling across the cement toward us.

We got to the boat and lay Harper on the deck. He was conscious but dazed. Blood from his nose stained the front of his sweater and his eyes seemed unfocussed.

Lucy grabbed the mooring rope and threw it aboard, following it quickly. Mike rushed into the cabin and started the engines.

As we backed away into deeper water, I risked a look at the zombies on the rocks.

There she was. Elena.

She stood at the water's edge. Her t-shirt was ripped and bloody, hanging off her in tatters. The left side of her neck was a big black gash, dark against her mottled blue skin. Her eyes glared at us with no recognition, only hunger. To her, we were no longer friends she had survived with. We simply prey.

"Oh, God," I whispered.

"I hope Mike doesn't see her," Lucy whispered back, closing her eyes as if she couldn't bear to see Elena like this any longer.

In the cabin, Mike stiffened. He looked at the herd of zombies. There was no way he didn't recognize Elena standing there.

He said nothing. Simply reversed the boat into deep water then turned her around and headed for the Big Easy.

"Should we mention it?" I asked Lucy.

"Only if he talks about it first. Otherwise, we keep quiet."

We sat silently in the back of the boat while Mike piloted us to the Big Easy.

He pulled up alongside the ladder and Lucy climbed out. As she ascended to the deck, Mike came over to me. There were tears in his eyes. He had seen Elena. No doubt about it. "Hey, Man, give me that flare gun so I can cover Harper."

I handed him the gun.

"And a flare, Man."

I gave him a flare. "You need any help with him?"

"Nah, he won't put up much of a fight. You get on board the Big Easy, Man."

I put a hand around the cold metal of the ladder. I turned to him. Something didn't feel right. "You OK, Mike?"

"I'm fine, Man."

I climbed the ladder and as I put my feet on the deck, I heard the engine of Harper's boat rev up. Mike piloted the craft out into the water off our stern.

He started taking the caps off the petrol cans and pouring the liquid over the boat.

"Mike, what are you doing?"

Lucy joined me at the railing. All we could do was watch as Mike doused Harper's boat in petrol.

"Mike!" Lucy shouted.

He ignored us, his eyes fixed on the zombies on the rocks as he covered the deck with gasoline. The smell reached us, so strong I felt like retching.

"Oh my God, Alex, stop him!" Lucy pleaded.

There was nothing I could do. Mike loaded the flare into the flare gun and went into the cabin, revving the engine and giving the boat full throttle.

Harper realized what was happening and his face turned into a pale mask of horror. "No!" he screamed, "No!"

The noise attracted the zombies on the rocks. They came to the water's edge, reaching out for the boat speeding toward them.

Elena stood with them. Mike aimed the boat for her.

Lucy's hands flew to her face and she turned away, unable to watch.

Harper continued screaming, fully aware that he was hurtling to his death.

As Mike got within twenty feet of the rocks, he fired the flare at the deck.

The boat became a fireball.

It hit the rocks and went off like a molotov cocktail.

The flaming hull split apart on the rocks and flaming gasoline spilled onto the zombies in burning torrents.

The boat exploded.

I didn't know how many zombies had been destroyed. There must have ben twenty at least.

One of them was Elena.

I closed my eyes and felt tears stinging my cheeks.

She and Mike now rested in peace.

Black smoke curled up into the grey sky from the rocks around the lighthouse. The smell of burning flesh filled the air.

Leaving Lucy curled up and sobbing on the aft deck, I climbed to the bridge and started our engines.

We had to get away from this place.

Twenty-six

FOR TWO DAYS, EVERYTHING WAS a blur.

I somehow managed to pilot the Big Easy North, keeping to the deep water well away from the coastline.

Lucy and I barely ate, barely communicated. We lived onboard the Big Easy like ghosts. Our existence felt ethereal, illusory. I knew we were in shock. The events since the virus outbreak had finally caught up with us. Our minds needed time to process all we had been through.

Even though I knew we were in shock, there was nothing I could do about it. I couldn't tell myself to just 'snap out of it'. My best friend was dead. Nothing would change that cold fact.

The weather closed in and I dropped anchor, leaving the boat bobbing on the waves as the tombstone sky cried down unending tears of rain all around us. The water-smeared windows offered us a view of sea and sky and rain and nothing else, adding to the illusion that none of this was real. Maybe I would wake up from this bad dream and Mike and Elena would still be alive. Maybe I would wake up in the tent in the mountains and none of this would have happened. All a dream. A stupid dream brought on by trying to keep up with Mike, Elena and Lucy as we hiked across the Welsh mountains.

On the third day, I lay on my bed staring at the ceiling. The wind had died down and the boat rocked gently on the water. I didn't know what time it was but the sky beyond the porthole was black. For the first time since Mike's death, I felt hungry.

If Lucy and I didn't take care of ourselves, this boat would become our floating tomb. I thought of Max Prentice lying on his bed in the Hornet, floating somewhere out at sea just like us. Would that be my fate? Lying on this bed forever while the Big Easy sat dead in the water?

Mike wouldn't want this. He wouldn't want us to give up.

I had been withdrawn for three days but now I craved human contact. I needed to hear Lucy's voice, touch her, know she was alive. We were both alive.

Alive.

The apocalypse had happened but we were still alive.

Survivors.

She must have felt the same need for contact because the bedroom door opened and she stood there wearing only her 'Sail To Your Destiny' t-shirt. I remembered the time at Doug Latimer's barbecue when she had stood in front of the refrigerator and taken a swig of beer, her breasts pushing against her black sweater. She looked that good to me right now as she stood in the doorway.

"Can I lie down with you?" she asked.

It felt good just to hear her voice. I nodded and moved back on the bed to give her room to lie with me.

She lay down in front of me, her back pressed against my chest, the curve of her bottom snug against the front of my boxers.

I placed my hand on her waist, feeling the warmth of her skin through the t-shirt. I could see the vein in her neck pulsing with life. She smelled of perspiration and tears. Her long hair caressed my face.

"We're alive," I said.

"Yes, we are."

My hand stroked her hip and she pressed herself back against me.

She was soft and exciting.

I kissed the pulsing vein on her neck and she turned her head so our lips met. After living through the end of the world, after drifting like ghosts for three days, we each desperately needed something that only the other could provide: human touch.

My hand explored the soft flesh of her thigh before moving up under the t-shirt to find the curves of her breasts. She moaned into my mouth as my fingers brushed her nipples.

It was a long night on the gentle waves and all movement, sound and touch merged into a single vivid dream of heat, tightness, sensation, and pleasure.

* * *

When I woke up, I could hear music.

Lucy was gone from the bed. We had fallen asleep together sometime in the night and the physical closeness had been like a life raft keeping us sane after all we had experienced. I listened to the music drifting down from the upper deck. Total Eclipse Of The Heart. An old song written in a different era but it still lifted my spirits. I sang along badly as I got out of bed. Through the porthole, the sky was blue and the clouds were white and unthreatening.

A good day for zombies.

I pushed that thought away and dressed hurriedly. The smell of bacon reached me and made my mouth water. We had found a freezer stocked with meat on the day we first boarded the Big Easy. We had agreed to only use it in special occasions as it was irreplaceable. Lucy had obviously decided that today was a special occasion.

I went up and found her in the kitchen leaning over the frying pan. She had a pan of beans on the stove and bread in the toaster. The smells assailing my nose were incredible.

"Something smells good," I said as I watched the bacon sizzling in the pan.

She looked over at me and smiled. "We need to keep our strength up if we're going to find those U.N. ships."

We hadn't talked about the rescue mission for the past three days. It had seemed unimportant... distant. Now we were ready to be rescued. It was the only way we were going to have a future that didn't involve violence and death.

After Bonnie Tyler finished singing, Johnny Drake came on the radio . "Hey to all the survivors out there. Here's a tune from way back when. The Doors and Strange Days." The music filled the room.

After three days of barely existing, the music and the smell of the food and the renewed sense of a goal was almost sensory overload. I sat in the easy chair and let myself become accustomed to this sudden influx of sensation.

The only depressing part of the morning was when the Survivor Reach Out segment came on the radio while we were eating our breakfast. More lost souls looking for their fellow lost souls. I saw a TV program once where the mother of a murder victim whose body was never found had said that not knowing was worse than knowing her son was dead. For these people on the radio, they would probably never know what had happened to their families and that would probably haunt them for the rest of their lives.

After three survivors told their stories and appealed for their relatives to get in contact with the nearest Survivors Camp, Johnny Drake's mellow voice came back on air. "Let's remember what we're surviving for, people. It's all about family."

After we had eaten, I went down to the shower and stood beneath the hot spray for fifteen minutes, letting the water roll over every inch of skin. Feeling cleansed, I went to the store room and picked out a new t-shirt. It had no logo, just a drawing of a yacht sailing into the sunset. The nautical folk sure liked their romanticism. I put on jeans and my boots and went up to the bridge while Lucy went below to have her shower.

The day was warm. In the distance, gulls cried. The sea undulated rhythmically as if it were breathing. The entire world seemed alive. *We* were alive.

I started the engine and pulled up the anchor before turning the Big Easy North and giving her a little throttle. We sailed through the calm water easily.

Maybe later I would get the fishing rods from below and try fishing for our dinner. We had plenty of food all around us. All we had to do was catch it.

Half an hour later, Lucy appeared on deck wearing jeans and a black sweater. I wondered if it was the sweater she had been wearing at Doug Latimer's barbecue. She had washed her hair and it trailed damply over her shoulders. She placed the radio on the deck and waved up at me before taking a seat in the sun. I waved back. The sound of a Snow Patrol song drifted out of the radio.

For the first time in a long while, I felt like things might actually turn out OK. I wondered about the logistics of the rescue mission being mounted by the U.N. There was no way they could take all the survivors out of Britain in a single ship. If that was the case, the virus had hit harder than I thought possible. It was more likely that each Survivors Camp would go to the rendezvous point in turn as different ships arrived to take them to safety. The operation could take months. We had been worrying that we might miss the rescue as if it were a single event. Now that I thought about it, that was a ridiculous notion. There would be plenty of ships, coming and going over a span of weeks. We would be able to get onboard one of them even if it meant going to a Survivors Camp for a week to be quarantined. That idea left a sour taste in my mouth but if it meant being rescued and starting a new life away from all of this, it was worth it.

* * *

We spent two weeks drifting off the coast of Scotland.

I managed to refuel the Big Easy at a deserted marina on the coast. The operation was carried out during heavy rain to protect us from zombies but even so, Lucy stood guard with the Colt while I figured out how to fill the tanks. We didn't run into any trouble and we avoided the temptation to search the marine store there. We simply refuelled and left.

I found a hard-covered notebook in one of the cupboards and I spent most evenings writing the story of our survival from the time I felt like I was dying in the Welsh mountains to the present day. It was hard to write about Mike and Elena now they were dead but the experience helped me deal with some of the grief I had been holding inside.

We listened to the radio every day hoping that Johnny Drake might mention the rescue mission but he never did. The Reach Out appeals didn't mention it either. Nobody said, "We're going to the rescue boats." They just asked their relatives to contact the army or the nearest Survivors Camp. Despite the sadness we felt every time the Reach Out was broadcast, the music that played in between those broadcasts was a constant companion and made us feel like we were still part of the world.

No ships arrived in Scotland as far as we could tell. I spent hours on the bridge scanning the sea with the high-powered binoculars. A few times I saw smaller boats like our own in the distance but I didn't hail them or approach them. The memories of the Hornet meant I wouldn't be boarding any strange vessels unless it was an emergency.

I searched the radio frequencies for transmissions from American ships but all I got was dead air.

Lucy spent the days reading paperbacks from the bookshelves and keeping stock of our food supplies. She also fished off the back off the boat. She wrote in her own journal in the evenings but I had no idea what she put in there.

We spent the nights entwined together in the bed.

I started to wonder if the rescue was ever going to happen.

I even wondered if I wanted it to.

We were surviving well and we were independent of any military control. I wasn't sure I wanted to give that up. Out here, we were in control of our lives. If we became part of a U.N. rescue mission, we would become refugees. Our future *might* be safe but at what cost to our freedom?

I distrusted authority. I always had. The thought of putting my life in their hands made something deep inside me rebel.

As far as post-apocalypse life went, ours was pretty good. I was sure there were plenty of people on the mainland fighting to survive a living hell. What would they give to be out here at sea on a comfortable boat, eating fresh fish and not worrying about zombies? Were we really going to give all that up?

The answer came one afternoon when I was looking through the binoculars and I spotted a luxury yacht in the distance. It wasn't the first time I had seen a boat through the high-powered lenses but something about this boat was different.

She was flying the stars and stripes.

Twenty-seven

I CALLED DOWN TO LUCY. She was sitting on the aft deck reading in the sun.

"There's an American boat over there." I pointed at the speck in the distance.

She shielded her eyes from the sun and peered across the water. "I don't see it."

"It's some way off. Should we go over there?"

"What for?"

"If the crew are American, they might know something about the rescue mission."

She shrugged. "I guess so."

I hadn't spoken to Lucy about my reluctance at getting rescued but it seemed to me that she was having similar thoughts. "We don't have to go," I said.

"No, we'll check it out. But we have to be careful OK?"

I grabbed the baseball bat I kept on the bridge and shook it in the air. "No fear. Me mighty warrior."

She rolled her eyes. "I'll get the gun."

I grinned and gunned the engines, turning the Big Easy around so she pointed directly at the American yacht.

* * *

Her name was 'Solstice' and she looked like she was worth a million dollars. Sitting proud and sleek on the ocean, she had an aft deck, a foredeck and an upper deck as well as a deck just above water level for swimming and diving. Her hull was dotted with portholes but her upper windows were made of tinted curved glass, running almost the entire length of the cabin. A table and chairs were set out on the aft deck.

I couldn't see any life on board. No movement.

Maybe they were all inside.

On a warm day like today? I doubted it.

A chill gripped my insides. This was like the Hornet all over again except on a larger scale. There could be a dozen people on that cruiser... or a dozen zombies. I suddenly felt that Lucy and I were vulnerable. Just two of us armed with a gun and a baseball bat. If the Solstice was full of zombies, we wouldn't have a chance. And what were we risking our lives for? News of a rescue that neither of us was sure we wanted to be a part of?

Lucy joined me on the bridge. "See anything?"

I handed her the binoculars. "I can't see anybody on board."

"Looks deserted."

"Yeah, maybe we should just ignore her."

She looked at me closely. "I thought we wanted information about the rescue."

"Do we?"

"What do you mean?"

"Do we really want to be rescued and shipped off to somewhere with everyone else?"

"I thought that was what we wanted." She hesitated then said, "Isn't it?" There was doubt in her voice.

"I'm not so sure anymore."

She put the binoculars down and sighed. "I know what you mean. At least we're in control of our own lives. But we should check out this boat. Even if we get some information, we don't have to act on it."

I agreed and brought the Big Easy around so we were headed for the diving deck on the stern of the Solstice. The only sound as we approached was Eminem coming from our radio. There was no point turning it off; we were hardly going to sneak up on the Solstice in a forty-two foot yacht. If anyone was on board, they would be aware of our presence by now.

Lucy jumped down onto the diving deck and tied us onto it. I cut our engine and climbed over the side of the Big Easy, dropping down onto the deck. The music coming from our boat had switched to an eighties pop tune. I didn't know where Johnny Drake got his music from but his playlist was definitely eclectic.

We went up the steps to the aft deck. The circular table and chairs in the center of the deck were arranged neatly, as was the rest of the craft from what I could see. Double glass doors led into a neat living room lined with leather sofas and chairs. A flat screen TV on the wall showed a black screen. There was nobody in there.

I relaxed my grip on the baseball bat slightly.

We knew the decks were deserted so if anyone was on board, they were beyond the living room. I opened the door and took a hesitant sniff of the air inside.

Rancid. Foul. I gagged and put my head back outside to breathe fresh air.

There were dead people in there. Maybe undead. If there was ever a good time to turn back, this was it.

"Do you really want to go in there?" I asked Lucy. "There's obviously nobody alive on this boat."

"We could go a little further. I've got the gun. We're OK." She stepped over the threshold and into the living area… if it could be called that anymore.

Breathing shallowly to smell as little of the fetid air as possible, I followed.

We found them in the kitchen. A family of four. They were all sat around the table as if they were gathered for a family meal. In fact, that was exactly what they had been doing. In front of each body was a half-eaten meal of mashed potatoes, peas, steak and gravy. Everyone had a glass of grape Kool-Aid poured from a pitcher that sat on the kitchen counter.

Mom and Dad looked like they were in their late thirties. Dad, whose body had sagged in his chair and whose mouth hung open, was dressed in a light blue polo shirt and white trousers. His hair was neat and he looked like he may have worked as a CEO for some company or other.

Mom had definitely been pretty. In fact, she was still pretty even in death. Her hair was long and auburn, spilling over her shoulders. Her make-up was applied perfectly and her face had the striking type of features that were usually found on models. She wore a yellow sun dress and apart from the fact that she was slumped to one side and her eyes were closed, you wouldn't know she was dead.

The children, a blonde girl who looked about ten and a hazelnut-headed boy of maybe twelve, had fallen forward and their heads rested on the table beside their plates.

"What do you think happened?" Lucy whispered.

"I don't know. Poison maybe? There aren't any marks on them. I'd say either the dad or the mom or both of them together poisoned their family. Maybe it's in the Kool-Aid or the food. Or both."

Her face looked horrified. "But why?"

I shrugged. I had no answer to that. The world had taken a sharp curve into madness but these people were removed from all that, just as we were. They were living in luxury. People have different tolerance levels and the situation must have become more than they could bear.

We explored the rest of the boat and found a laptop computer in the master bedroom. It was still plugged in and had power. I swished my finger across the mousepad and the screen came to life. The computer had been on the internet. The browser window had a number of tabs open, each showing the last page viewed. All were News websites.

The headline on the page that was open told the story.

VIRUS OUTBREAK IN THE U.S.

I clicked on one of the tabs to find a second News site.

PRESIDENT DECLARES STATE OF EMERGENCY.

There were eight sites open and they all said pretty much the same thing. The virus had reached America. The U.S. Military were fighting hordes of zombies in almost every state. Society was collapsing.

This was why no one had come for us.

The dead were rising all over the world.

There was nobody left to mount a rescue mission.

"Nowhere is safe," Lucy whispered.

I closed the laptop and unplugged it. "We might as well take this with us."

She nodded.

"Is there anything else you want to take?" I asked her.

She shook her head. "No." Tears pooled in her eyes.

We walked past the dead family and out to our boat. Somebody in there... either the father or the mother... had read those news reports and then decided to cook one last meal for the family. Maybe the parents had decided to do it together and sat their calmly with their kids eating a meal that they knew would kill them.

They were free from the apocalypse now. No more struggle for survival. No more fear.

We got back onto the Big Easy and I put the laptop on the coffee table in the living room. I didn't want to look at it right now. I just wanted to get away from this death boat and into open water where I could forget that the whole world had gone to hell and just feel the breeze on my face and listen to music from a better time.

Lucy untied us and jumped aboard and I pulled away from the Solstice on a heading that would take us South to warmer waters. There was no point staying in Scottish waters if there were no rescue ships coming. We might as well sail into better weather and warmer climes off the coast of Cornwall. It didn't matter anymore.

I gave the Big Easy more throttle and I felt better when the Solstice diminished to a dark shape on the waves, then a speck, then nothing as we got too far away to see her. I kept us out in deep water, not wanting to be anywhere near the coast when we passed the lighthouse. I didn't want to see that place ever again.

I wondered what the military were going to do with the Survivors Camps now that there was no rescue planned. I expected the British government, safe somewhere in an underground bunker, had plans for the civilians. Whatever they were, I wanted no part of them. The Big Easy was home now and as long as we could avoid pirates and military ships, this was where we would stay.

I felt optimistic about the future.

All of that changed when a familiar voice floated up to me from the deck below.

"My name is Joe Harley and I'm looking for my brother Alex."

Joe. It was Joe! "Oh my God that's my brother!" I slid down the ladder to the deck and turned up the radio. Lucy came out from the living room, a look of surprise on her face.

"...was camping with his friends in Wales when all of this happened. So we're hoping he's OK. We can't find him on the Survivor Board but he might not be in a camp. He doesn't like the army or police. That's just Alex, you know. Anyway, Alex, if you're out there, we're all OK. Mom and Dad are here too. Get in contact if you can. Say hello to Mike from us. We love you."

Hot stinging tears rolled down my cheeks.

It was Joe.

He was alive.

Somewhere out there, Joe was alive. And Mom and Dad too.

Alive.

"Oh my God," I said, crying into my hands.

Lucy put an arm around me. "I'm so happy for you, Alex. They're safe."

They were in a camp. They had somehow ended up in a camp. That wasn't safe. Out here, *this* was safe. The camps weren't safe. Once the millions of zombies left the cities in search of more victims, they would travel into the countryside where the military had set up the camps. Huge concentrations of people would draw their attention. They would overwhelm the survivors by sheer numbers. Joe and my parents wouldn't stand a chance. They were fenced in somewhere in a military compound and it was only a matter of time before the zombies got to them.

"I have to go and get them," I said, looking toward the distant mainland.

"What? Alex, you can't be serious. You have no idea where they are."

"He mentioned something about a Survivor Board. If I can find out what that is, it might tell me where I can find them."

"You know how many zombies there are on the mainland. This is crazy!"

"I have to do it."

I climbed back up onto the bridge and turned the Big Easy toward the shore. I remembered the first dream I had on this boat, a dream of sailing across miles of ocean to reach an island plagued by zombies.

Now it was going to be real.

No longer just a dream.

A living nightmare.

*

THE END

13797988R00134

Printed in Great Britain
by Amazon.co.uk, Ltd.,
Marston Gate.